**"Go home, Alek," she said, quickly moving to the front door to open it wide.**

"I will," he said, coming to stand before her. "But this thing between us will happen one day. I will make love to you, Alessandra, and we will enjoy it together."

She stepped back and felt for the door, taking a deep swallow as she released a shaky breath.

He stepped close to her. She wanted him just as badly as he wanted her. It was hard to miss. The hot eyes, bated breath and gaping mouth. "It's better sooner than later so we can get it out of our systems and focus on work, right? You're just as curious as I am. Will it be as good as we think?"

Alessandra's eyes dropped to his mouth and lingered there.

"Is curiosity killing that cat?" he taunted softly, his breath fanning against her mouth from their closeness.

She pouted before she released a little cry of alarm as she turned her head to keep them from kissing.

He turned to stride away.

Alessandra reached out for him. "Yes, it is," she answered.

D0249358

Dear Reader,

I'm a romantic at heart, and nothing pleases me more than romance novels set in small towns. While creating my new series, Passion Grove, centered on a very affluent small town built around a heart-shaped lake, I knew I would enjoy writing stories of love and passion with such an ideal setting.

After thirty books in print, I also wanted to try something different with the characters, and what better way to let my imagination fly than making them ultrawealthy? Beautiful billionaires who have it all when it comes to money, but are still unable to find love—the most important thing to cherish.

I hope *A Billionaire Affair* is as much fun to read as it was for me to write. It's bursting with chemistry, conflict, passion and, ultimately, a deep, lasting love that will make you root for happily-ever-after.

To find out more, visit me at www.niobiabryant.com, or my Facebook fan page—Niobia Bryant | Meesha Mink.

Written with every bit of my belief in love,

*Niobia*

# A BILLIONAIRE Affair

Niobia Bryant

HARLEQUIN® KIMANI™ ROMANCE

If you purchased this book without a cover you should be aware that this book is stolen property. It was reported as "unsold and destroyed" to the publisher, and neither the author nor the publisher has received any payment for this "stripped book."

Recycling programs for this product may not exist in your area.

ISBN-13: 978-1-335-21665-6

A Billionaire Affair

Copyright © 2018 by Niobia Bryant

All rights reserved. The reproduction, transmission or utilization of this work in whole or in part in any form by any electronic, mechanical or other means, now known or hereafter invented, including xerography, photocopying and recording, or in any information storage or retrieval system, is forbidden without written permission. For permission please contact Harlequin Kimani, 22 Adelaide St. West, 40th Floor, Toronto, Ontario M5H 4E3, Canada.

This is a work of fiction. Names, characters, places and incidents are either the product of the author's imagination or are used fictitiously, and any resemblance to actual persons, living or dead, business establishments, events or locales is entirely coincidental.

® and TM are trademarks of Harlequin Enterprises Limited or its corporate affiliates. Trademarks indicated with ® are registered in the United States Patent and Trademark Office, the Canadian Intellectual Property Office and in other countries.

For questions and comments about the quality of this book please contact us at CustomerService@Harlequin.com.

HARLEQUIN®
www.Harlequin.com

Printed in U.S.A.

**Niobia Bryant** is the award-winning and national bestselling author of more than thirty works of romance and commercial mainstream fiction. Twice she has won the RT Reviewers' Choice Best Book Award for African-American/Multicultural Romance. Her most recent book written under the pseudonym of Meesha Mink was listed as one of *Library Journal*'s Best Books of 2014 in the African American fiction category. Her books have appeared in *Ebony*, *Essence*, the *New York Post*, *The Star-Ledger*, *The Dallas Morning News* and many other national publications. Her bestselling book was adapted to film.

"I am a writer, born and bred. I can't even fathom what else I would do besides creating stories and telling tales. When it comes to my writing I dabble in many genres, my ideas are unlimited and the ink in my pen is infinite." —Niobia Bryant

---

**Books by Niobia Bryant**

**Harlequin Kimani Romance**

*A Billionaire Affair*

As always, for my mama, my guardian angel,
Letha "Bird" Bryant.

# Chapter 1

"Have a good evening, sir."

Alek Ansah nodded sharply at the pilot and crew of his private plane just before disembarking. Quickly he jogged down the metal stairs, not even paying attention to the crisp London night air whipping against the hand-tailored tuxedo on his well-built frame. He checked his de Grisogono watch as he strode across the airfield to his waiting black Bentley Mulsanne. By the time he reached it, his longtime driver had exited the vehicle and held the rear door open.

"Julius," Alek greeted him, his accent a blend of his Ghanaian ancestry and his upbringing in England. He unbuttoned his jacket and slid onto the smooth leather seat.

"Sir." His driver gave him a polite nod of his head.

As soon as the door closed, Alek relaxed and settled his chin in his hand as he released a heavy breath and looked out the darkly tinted window as the vehicle eased forward. The sights of London were reflected in the depths of his coal-black eyes. The capital of both England and the United Kingdom had served as his home base for the last five years.

That would change tomorrow.

Alek was surprised at the slight tinge of nervousness he felt. Was it leftover anxiety about the fear of flying that he hid so well, or the day of reckoning fast approaching? He sighed, his mood now pensive.

The ride from the airport to his penthouse apartment in the heart of historical and prestigious Westminster took less than fifteen minutes. As the car rolled to a smooth stop outside the building constructed of stone, granite and bronze, Alek looked up at the illuminated floor-to-ceiling windows of his apartment. It was the lone flat on the tenth floor.

He climbed from the vehicle before Julius could even leave his seat. "Good night, Julius," Alek called over his shoulder, already loosening his bow tie and the top button of his monogrammed shirt as he strolled up the length of the walkway and entered the building.

After a full day of work topped with his evening flight to and from Paris just to attend a charity event at the Pavillon d'Armenonville, his muscles felt weak with fatigue—a rarity for him. He was strong and fit and thrived on challenge. Still, he was human and required even minimal rest.

Striding across the stylishly appointed lobby, the soles of his handmade Italian shoes beat against the marble floors as he made his way to the elevators. He entered his private code for the elevator to go to the penthouse and rode in silence. As he stood there with his legs apart and his hands behind his back, he flexed his shoulders and rolled his head to relieve the slight strain of tension he felt. He paused when he caught sight of his reflection against the bronze of the double doors.

He did a double take and then chuckled a bit. Earlier that night one of the waitresses shared with him that he should audition to be the first black James Bond. He was nearly 100 percent sure she thought he was Idris Elba. He didn't know whether to be flattered by that or insulted that he was the honoree at the very event where she worked and she had no clue who he was. That was a first in the circles in which he moved.

The doors of the elevators opened directly into his apartment, he removed his white dinner jacket and folded it over the back of one of the four modern charcoal sofas in his expansive living room.

"Your drink, sir."

Alek turned away from the view of the London cityscape to find his loyal manservant, Huntsman, still very much awake, dressed in customary black on black attire and ready to serve. With a smile, he accepted the snifter of brandy from the small wooden tray held by the bald middle-aged man. The warmed crystal felt good in his hand as he swirled the alcohol and took a small sniff of the aromas released by the heating of the glass before taking a satisfying sip.

Over the rim of the glass, he looked out at the sight of Westminster Abbey and the Houses of Parliament in the distance. At night, he often found himself standing there in front of his windows enjoying the sight.

To think there was a time when none of it mattered to him. Simplicity had been key.

With a smirk, he looked around at his lavish surroundings. Everything had changed, and sometimes he wasn't sure it was for the better. With a slight clench of his square jaw, Alek focused on his six-foot reflection, letting the cityscape laid out before him blur as he did.

Sometimes he felt he hardly knew the man in the reflection.

"Big day tomorrow, sir."

With another sip, Alek glanced over his shoulder to find that Huntsman had never moved from his spot, the serving tray still in his hand. "Very," he agreed, curving his lips into a smile.

Huntsman chuckled.

The two had been officially employer and employee over the last fifteen of Alek's thirty years of life, but they had a friendship and a mutual respect that extended beyond a work relationship and their twenty-year age difference. Huntsman knew almost everything about Alek's life and pretended to turn a blind eye to his jet-setting ways filled with a string of beautiful women that gave the international paparazzi plenty on which to report. It was well documented that Alek Ansah worked hard, but he played just as hard.

Still, Huntsman was very aware of Alek's inner struggles, and he knew Alek's imminent return to New York was a mixed blessing.

"Your luggage and travel arrangements are prepared. Are you?" Huntsman asked, stepping up to stand beside him.

"I don't really have a choice, do I?" Alek asked, and took another deep sip.

"No, sir, you do not."

In the morning, Alek would return to the corporate headquarters of the Ansah Dalmount Group in New York to officially claim his position as the cochairman of the billion-dollar conglomerate. He was fulfilling the wishes of his father, Kwame Ansah, and not his own. "You won, Dad," he mouthed as he lifted his snifter in a toast and looked up to the heavens with a small sardonic shake of his head, as a wave of grief caused his gut to clench.

Five years ago, the lives of both his father and his father's business partner, Frances Dalmount, were tragically ended in a crash of ADG's company jet. He had been deep into his grief and grappling with the lost opportunity to mend his strained relationship with his father when the reading of the will completely turned Alek's life upside down.

Alek's grandfather, Ebo Ansah, began a financial services firm in Ghana in the 1950s that grew significantly in the mid-1960s, providing a very respectable living for his wife, Kessie, and their four children. His eldest son, Kwame, grew under the tutelage of his father and was anxious for his opportunity to enter the family business. They expanded the fiscal services offered to their loyal clients and grew their business. Life was good, and with the Ansah men working together doggedly, it became even better. Upon Ebo's passing in the early 1980s Kwame took over the running of the business, aggressively taking over smaller banks and insurance and investment firms to catapult himself to wealth and prominence. When the opportunity arose in 1987 to join forces with Frances Dalmount, a business competitor from England, he accepted with the intent to use their combined resources to take on other business ventures. The Ansah Dalmount Group was formed, eventually becoming one of the most successful conglomerates in the world with its business umbrella encompassing financial services, oil, hotels/resorts/casinos and telecommunications.

Kwame Ansah relished every moment of their success because he knew his father would be proud. And he wanted nothing more than for his eldest son to join him to advance the company even further. It was their biggest point of contention.

Alek clenched his jaw in regret.

After graduating with a Master of Business Administration degree from Columbia University, Alek did not enter the family business as planned and instead fostered his love of the outdoors and sailing by working as a deckhand on a luxury mega yacht, with plans to rise up the ranks to captain his own vessel. What his father saw as defiance was just him fighting for his independence to be his own man. It was the first time he ever defied him.

Back then he felt so much pride in striking out on his own.

Back then he was pleased that his job kept him away from home so that he could avoid the look of disappointment and anger in his father's eyes.

Back then he thought he had more time to make everything right.

And now?

Five years had passed and the guilt was still palpable.

"I knew your father well, Alek," Huntsman said,

reaching up with his free hand to firmly pat his shoulder. "You have already made him proud."

Alek's smile was slight but genuine. "He threw me in the deep end and I had no choice but to sink or swim," he said with a chuckle.

Kwame Ansah had been determined to have his way, even in death.

Alek had to make the difficult choice of accepting the position as cochief executive officer of ADG or having all his father's shares in the conglomerate sold, with the proceeds donated to various charities. That would leave not only Alek but the rest of his family without an inheritance. His father had to have known he would never lose the family's legacy and financial security. *Stubborn old man*

Kwame Ansah was relentless, and in the end, he had been right. Per his father's request he had spent the last five years training inside the company in preparation to run it. He spent considerable time within every branch of the ADG learning about it from the ground floor up. He took to it all like a fish to water. He soared, driven by a desire to make his father proud, but also pure determination to thrive and win—traits he inherited from his sire.

For so long, his stubbornness to pave his own path in life had blinded him to the innate skill and tenacity his father had seen in him all the while.

Now he was prepared to take the Ansah Dalmount Group even further.

*Well, along with Alessandra*, he conceded, sliding one hand into the pocket of his tailored slacks and taking another sip as he shook his head.

The news that his father's business partner had left

his shares of their billion-dollar conglomerate to his daughter had yet to sit well with him. Their power in the company was equal. Each inherited 49 percent of the shares, with the board of directors left with 2 percent of the shares to decide on a stalemate between them.

Alek felt that was inevitable.

They were completely driven.

With their fathers as both business associates and close friends, Alek had known Alessandra since childhood. Ever since they were small, Alek had found Alessandra's quiet nature off-putting. She was never friendly and seemed afraid of her own shadow. As teenagers, they were never in the same circle of friends or schools but saw each other at social functions. She was decidedly awkward and found with her head in a book more times than not. He had little patience for the mousy little introvert and was glad their time in each other's presence became nonexistent with age.

He frowned at the memory of her during their first meeting with the board of directors of ADG. Slender and petite with a head full of massive curls that dwarfed her face. Her petite figure swamped in the shirt and pants she wore. Oversize, ill-adjusted spectacles that she continuously pushed up on her nose. Nervously biting at her bottom lip. Looking confused, lost and unaware that she was completely out of her element.

He expressed his discontent with her appointment as co-CEO, so much so that the board readily agreed to his request to do his training in their London offices while Alessandra remained in New York. That was the last time he saw Miss Alessandra Dalmount.

And all of that would change tomorrow.

*Everything* would change tomorrow.

Alek released a heavy breath.

"It is not your last walk to the electric chair, sir," Huntsman said, taking the now-empty snifter from him to cross the polished floor to refill it.

Alek reached up to run his long fingers across his close-shaven head. It wasn't the move that Huntsman spoke of and they both knew it. It was not a "what" but a "whom."

Alessandra Dalmount.

He accepted the snifter Huntsman pressed into his hand. "What in the world was Frances thinking?" he muttered darkly, his brow furrowing as he gripped the nightcap so hard that a lesser material would have crushed in his grasp.

"Ah, the eternal question," Huntsman said softly, his tone amused.

"I will not sit back and let her destroy everything our fathers worked so hard to build," Alek said sharply, turning in his spot to face the older man.

Huntsman smoothed his hands over his vest before clasping his hands together behind his back and rapping his heels together. "And yet the firm still stands strong after five years of her working there," he said smoothly, his face almost unreadable.

"But she gains forty-nine percent control tomorrow—"

"As do you, sir," Huntsman reminded him.

"Yes, but *I* know what the hell I'm doing!" Alek snapped.

*Ding-dong.*

"Plans, sir?" Huntsman asked drily.

"Damn," Alek swore, dropping his head so low that his chin almost touched his chest.

He'd forgotten the beautiful woman he'd met after a business lunch out on the cigar terrace of the Boisdale of Belgravia earlier that day. It had been hard not to notice one of the few women enjoying the decidedly masculine Scottish decor, particularly her handling of the long and thick cigar in her mouth as she boldly met his stare from across the terrace. She'd made an invite back to his apartment for a nightcap completely undeniable.

He'd since forgotten all about her.

Huntsman waited patiently as Alek looked down into his drink and then toward the door before looking back at his drink again. Whatever desire he had to bed the woman had waned. He couldn't remember her name and could only vaguely recall her beauty.

"Have my driver take her home and offer her my apologies," Alek said before tipping his head back to finish his drink.

Huntsman immediately turned to do as he was bid.

Alek wasn't proud of treating the woman like a disposable convenience. It wasn't usually his character, but he would not be good company for her or anyone else that night. His thoughts were centered on one thing and one thing alone: how to convince Alessandra Dalmount to willingly step down from her position at ADG.

For him, that was *all* that mattered.

Alessandra Dalmount leaned back in her leather executive chair and crossed her legs in the pin-striped pencil skirt she wore as she coolly eyed the junior executives sitting in the leather club chairs across from her at the conference room table. The two young men glanced at each other and shifted nervously in their seats as her silence filled the air.

As she continued to study them, Alessandra took the moment to ponder how hard she had to fight to prove her worth in the last five years. She was proud to finally be so respected within the company that her silence after the presentation of a business proposal elicited subtle anxiety. In the early days of stepping into the role her father had bequeathed her, Alessandra had been nervous, fidgety and apologetic. She had felt so unsure in her role. So unworthy. So judged.

*Well, no more.*

"As you all know, the expansion of ADG into the shipping industry has been of the utmost importance to me for the last year," she began. "I expect some resistance."

*From Alek Ansah.*

She forced a stiff smile and nearly snapped the pen she held in half from her tightened grasp as she shifted in her seat. She forced herself to do a mental five count as her employees watched her.

*Get it together, Alessandra.*

"I expect my team to gather the information and analytics I need on the list of firms I am suggesting the company acquire. I will make some notations and corrections to the report and get them back to you this evening," she said, forcing her shoulders to relax as she stood up on her sling-back Fendi heels and gave each man a hard stare. "I expect the amended reports back to me before the end of the week, sans the little loopholes I've already discovered after a two-minute cursory perusal."

"But, Ms. Dalmount..." one of them said.

"That is all," Alessandra said firmly, dismissing them as she turned to look out the window at the Empire State Building among the sprawling landscape of Midtown Manhattan.

As her staff members quietly took their leave, her focus on the neighboring high-rise buildings blurred. She pursed her lips and released a breath meant to calm her nerves. It didn't work.

Today she would assume her share of the responsibility in running one of the largest conglomerates in the country. She had the last five years to prepare, but in this moment, she felt as if that time had flown by so quickly.

And in truth she felt completely overwhelmed.

Alessandra unclasped the locket she wore on a long chain around her neck and stroked her thumb against the wedding photo of her parents nestled there. They both were lost to her. Her mother, Olivia, died when Alessandra was young, and her father had loved his wife so deeply that he never remarried. She could only find solace that her parents had reunited in heaven.

*I miss you, Daddy.*

As always, the thought of her father dying in such a tragic way weakened her knees. She closed her eyes as a wave of sadness and grief hit her, causing her to wince. *Will the pain ever dull?*

Not enough time had passed to properly grieve the death of a parent. In the space of a week, she lost her father, attended the funeral and then learned during his will reading that it was his wish for her to take over his position as a chief executive officer of the Ansah Dalmount Group. She'd wanted nothing more than to return to their family estate and bury her head under the dozen pillows on her bed so that she could sleep and pretend the week had never happened.

But that wasn't to be.

Alessandra had been completely moved and surprised by her father's faith in her, but her fear of it all had come with a quickness. Although she had previously graduated with a bachelor's in English, Alessandra's life had been all about her volunteer work for various charities. With one stroke of his pen, Frances Dalmount had solidified his daughter as one of the most wealthy and powerful women in the world. And now the day had arrived for her to take the reins.

*Father, what have you gotten me into?*

Alessandra closed the locket but kept it pressed in her hand.

Back then the last thing she wanted was the responsibility of taking over the family empire. She had hardly ever bothered herself with her father's business affairs. She was his only child, and although he loved and spoiled her immensely, she had always known he would have preferred a son to raise in the ways of business. She had never held ill will about that.

And she never assumed he would expect so much of her.

Alessandra squeezed the bridge of her nose as she turned and walked along the length of the table to leave the modern and stylish conference room. Closing the glass door behind herself, she began walked down the hall to the right to her corner office, but stopped midway with a soft curving of her crimson-painted lips. Instead she turned and walked down the opposite end of the hall to the elevator. As the wood-paneled doors opened, she stepped on and pressed the button to go to the top floor of the twenty-five-story building.

She couldn't lie; there *was* excitement blended with her fear.

The last five years she worked hard to form herself into a successful businesswoman. Between the fifty- to sixty-hour weeks she put in working in various departments to garner a firsthand knowledge of the business, to returning to college to earn her Master of Business Administration from Columbia University, to reshaping her image and bolstering her confidence, Alessandra went above and beyond to prove herself to the naysayers. It was clear that many people questioned her father's decision to have her inherit his shares of ADG—she even questioned it herself.

Pain over her father's death, anger about being openly scorned because she was a woman and a desire to win motivated Alessandra.

And she had thrived. She surprised the board members and her peers. She took pride in that. Alessandra had given up so much to live up to what her father expected of her. *So very much.*

The elevator slowed to a stop and the doors slid open, revealing the wide reception area. To her left was a sandalwood station beneath the backlit brass letters *ADG* on the wall, and to the right sat a modern sofa with sleek lines. Her eyes quickly landed directly across from her on the ornate double doors of the palatial boardroom. She smoothed her hands down her hips and stiffened her spine as she walked off the elevator.

ADG owned the entire commercial building, leasing out all but the top four floors with the penthouse reserved just for the expansive offices of the two CEOs.

That morning when she arrived, she learned one of those offices was now hers.

The receptionist, a tall redhead with glasses, rose to her feet. "Good morning, Ms. Dalmount," she said with a warm smile.

Alessandra fought her natural inclination to return the smile and instead gave her a polite nod as she passed her to enter the wide hall. She paused and turned to look back at the hall to the right of the elevator, which led to the other office now belonging to Alek Ansah.

Her heart pounded and she nervously bit the gloss from her lips. *Is he in there?*

It had been five years since she'd seen him in person, and the last time would be hard to ever forget. Her father's attorney had announced, "Alessandra Dalmount and Alek Ansah, as the newly appointed majority owners of ADG, you will both be primed within the company to take over the running of the conglomerate—together."

Behind her spectacles she had looked to Alek. He had barely spared her a glance when he first entered the office and took the seat across from her, but his dark eyes were locked and loaded on her. His square and handsome chiseled features had been unreadable, but his eyes told the story: he was not happy with having her as his equal.

Their fathers had been competitors before becoming business partners and eventually best friends. Alessandra had known Alek since they were children, although they encountered each other more as teenagers. As they moved into adulthood, she watched the surly teen grow into an arrogant and cocky man. His demeanor toward her had always been decidedly brooding, but bordered on hostile when he discovered they would run ADG together.

*It's been five years; does he feel the same?*

She fought the urge to ask Emily if he was in fact in his office. The board meeting was tomorrow morning and she would undoubtedly see him then. Alessandra flipped her straight hair over her shoulder as she arched a brow and released a heavy breath. If he was still unwilling to accept her role in the company, then, like their offices, they would remain at opposite ends. *The choice is his to make.*

Sighing, she continued down the hall, her heels echoing against the marble floor. The glass door leading into the outer office automatically opened upon her approach. Unger Rawlings, her executive assistant, instantly rose to his feet and grabbed his iPad, but she held up her hand and softly shook her head to prevent him from following her through the open double doors into her office. "I'm fine for now, Unger," she assured him.

"Yes, ma'am."

He had been her right-hand man and dedicated employee since her first day at ADG. The tall and slender young man, who was just a little younger than her thirty years, knew all too well of her priorities. She could think of no one else to serve as her assistant, even if there had been a push for someone with more experience and qualifications. His professionalism and loyalty were significant to her.

"Actually, you can go to lunch, Unger," she said.

"Would you like anything?" he asked.

She shook her head.

It was solace that she sought.

Alessandra paused in the doorway and took in the nearly 360-degree view of Manhattan through the three glass curtain walls of her office. The open floor plan was breathtakingly beautiful and sleek with over three thousand square feet, twenty-foot ceilings with skylights, private spa bath, small kitchen, exercise room, lounge area with a grand fireplace, library and an outdoor terrace. All was stylishly designed in luxury, but it wasn't the grandeur of the space that caused her to pause.

Although the office had been updated and remodeled in the last five years, to her it was still her father's space and he was gone.

"Deep thoughts?"

Alessandra froze. She didn't need to see the face that matched the seductive, masculine voice. It had been years, but she knew it well. Hating the feeling of nervous anxiety that plagued her as his return became imminent, she stiffened her spine and prayed her makeup and hair were still flawless. *Keep it cool.*

"Welcome back, Alek," she said coolly, slowly walking the length of the polished hardwood floors to reach her large desk. She turned to face him, leaning back against the edge of her desk and crossing her ankles.

There he stood in the open doorway in a designer suit and handmade shoes, looking every bit the man of power. Polished. Stylish. Tall, truly dark and unapologetically handsome. Black hair cut low, dark eyes, bronzed brown complexion. His groomed beard emphasized his high cheekbones and square jawline. He stood right at six feet tall with a strong, athletic build that his tailored suit couldn't hide.

Alessandra's eyes missed nothing, not even the small scar on his cheek that added a dangerous edge to his style. She had always considered him a fine-looking man, but the years made him more rugged… more handsome.

*Sexy. Too damn sexy.*

Alessandra had heard of and seen Alek's personal life in the press, but the photos of him and his rotation of beautiful dates had not prepared her for all of him in person. Her facade was cool as she hid her pounding heart and racing pulse. Alek Ansah was pure, raw sex appeal.

*Well, I'll be damned.*

"Alessandra," he said, his voice deep and rich with that British accent.

*Boom-boom-boom-boom-boom.*

Alessandra's heart betrayed her. She ignored the almost deafening pounding as she eyed him strolling into her office. He came over to stand at her window, his coal-black eyes locked on some spot in the distance. He had the kind of stride that hinted at his sexual prowess.

She looked back over her shoulder. Her eyes caressed his profile. *Sexy arrogant bully.*

Alek suddenly turned his head to eye her, as well.

Alessandra kept her face nonchalant. "Can I help you with something, Alek?" she asked, rising to come around her desk and pull back her chair to claim her seat behind it. Her hand was as unsteady as her pulse as she picked up her favorite Aurora fountain pen.

"There are whispers in the air that you are proposing working on a deal to shift the firm into shipping," he said, moving over to stand in front of her desk.

Alessandra glanced up at him, purposely dismissing him with her eyes as she pretended to focus on the files and forms before her. "Whispers, Alek?" she said mockingly. "I would think a man like you was above listening to...whispers."

"A man like me, Alessandra?"

She allowed herself a moment to close her eyes at how his tongue seemed to caress her name. Dropping her pen, she leaned back in her chair and looked up at him. "Your first day back and we're picking—no, no, no—*you're* picking up right where you left off," she said with a disapproving twist of her lips.

"My feelings haven't changed since my last day here," he assured her, his eyes locked on her.

"Your feelings about me, I assume?" Alessandra rose to her feet, hating the feeling of him looking down on her.

"Exactly."

She felt affronted. "And your issue with me is?" she asked, deciding to be just as bold as him.

"Your refusal to step down from a position not suited

for you," he instantly shot back with ease as if the words had been sitting perched on the tip of his tongue.

"It's too bad you feel that way, Alek," she said, her voice firm. "Because you're mistaken."

His eyes took her in. Her hair. Her face. The fit of the embroidered satin shirt she wore with a formfitting pencil skirt. A warm appreciation filled the dark depths.

In the years since she blossomed into a swan, she had learned to pick up on the unspoken cues of a man. She felt desired at his perusal, but his demeanor toward her was weakening her desire of him.

Alek reached across the desk dividing them to stroke her hair. "I like your new look. Playing dress-up?" he asked, slightly mocking.

She held his stare as she coolly raised her hand to brush away his touch. "Change is good, Alek. Particularly change of times. Why don't you and your outdated chauvinistic thinking join the rest of us in the current year."

"This should be fun," Alek said, nodding his head and smiling.

"Games are not a part of my day, Alek," she snapped. "I will not be undermined in this business by you and your return. I have earned my MBA from your alma mater. I have worked my way up inside this business. I have implemented deals that have generated ADG a steady influx of money. I have proved my worth. And, most importantly, *Alek*, I own the same number of shares as you. We are equals. And I'm not going anywhere."

He wiped his mouth as he eyed her with a hint of

amusement in his eyes. “We’ll see,” he said simply before turning to walk out of her office.

Even as his arrogance burned her gut, her eyes took in his smooth stride until he disappeared from her line of vision. Forcing herself to relax, she dropped down into her seat and swiveled to look out the window at the Manhattan views as she attempted to release her anger and her desire.

# *Chapter 2*

*What a difference five years makes.*

Alek picked up his crystal glass of water and closely watched Alessandra over the rim as she spoke to the board members from her seat at the opposite end of the conference table. Where once she had been an ineffectual woman who seemed afraid of her own shadow, her slender face buried beneath a ton of curls and so thin that the wind could shift her like a leaf, she had transformed herself both physically and in temperament. The dull caterpillar had become a jewel-toned butterfly.

Her dark tresses were bone straight and expertly styled to complement her heart-shaped face and caramel-brown complexion. Makeup highlighted her almond-shaped eyes of brandy, blush contoured her high cheekbones, and gloss made her full lips poutier and succulent. Her height was average but the curves of her toned shape were not. She wore a dark gray chiffon blouse with sheer sleeves and a plunging neckline that was just deep enough to allude to more without revealing it. She paired it with wide-leg pants that fit close against her hips before falling straight to the floor and flaring. Her outfit was professional with a sexy edge.

His eyes dipped down to her mouth as she spoke. He liked the way the tip of her tongue caressed the small dip in the center of her bottom lip. Her oxblood lipstick gave her a dramatic flair that was hard to ignore.

Alek took a deep sip of water as he forced himself to look away from her. To not be drawn into her, into everything she had become: a mix of cool confidence and simmering sex appeal. He definitely enjoyed the look of her more than what she was saying.

"Alek… Alek…your thoughts?"

He blinked away a vision of undoing every button of Alessandra's shirt to bury his head against her breasts as he pressed her body down onto the conference table. His eyes shifted to Aldrich Brent, the president of the corporation and executive board member. "I'm not impressed," he said dismissively, rising to his feet. He smoothed his double-knotted silk tie before buttoning the jacket of his custom Tom Ford pin-striped suit. "It's clear that Alessandra is naive and amateurish in business. I am disappointed she felt competent in presenting this venture to the board."

Alessandra mumbled under her breath.

He offered her a brief glance as he reached for his briefcase and pulled a stack of twelve black folders from it. "I would like to offer an alternative that is *viable*," he stressed, walking around the table to place a report before each of the ten board members flanking the table and then Alessandra sitting at the end opposite him.

She took it from him with a hard stare.

He came to stand next to his seat at the end of the table. “Anyone with an iota of business acumen could ascertain—”

“Enough of the insults, Alek,” Alessandra requested calmly.

He feigned confusion. “Insults?” he asked.

“Yes, less of them and more of your proposal is all that I’m asking,” she said.

Only the fire in her eyes revealed her rising ire at him.

“Do you need a moment?” he asked, his tone mocking as he egged her on.

Her mouth tightened into a thin line and her jaw was clenched so tightly that he was sure she could bite a nail in half with ease.

Alek cleared his throat. “The interest of ADG would be better served with a move into commercial aviation,” he said.

“Commercial aviation,” Alessandra snapped, tossing the folder on the table where it spun like a top until it hit against a board member’s glass of water.

“Yes,” he answered, his gaze leveling on her. Her annoyance with him caused her eyes to shine brightly. He forced himself to look away from her as he felt his usual cool composure wane. *When did she become so beautiful?*

“And we’re supposed to believe this is not just a last-minute stunt to gun for my venture idea?” she asked coldly.

"Yes."

Alessandra swore, and then winced in regret. Such language wasn't appropriate, no matter the impetus.

The chaotic energy around them seemed to whip loudly in the air with the force of lightning.

"Really?" Alek asked, his tone scolding.

"My apologies, but as you all can see nothing has changed between Mr. Ansah and me since our last meeting in this boardroom five years ago," she explained, her tone calm and composed.

The board members and the secretary taking the notes stirred in their seats as Alessandra and Alek cast each other cold glares.

"Very unprofessional, Alessandra," Alek said with a smugness at her losing her equanimity. He wasn't finished. "The boardroom is no place for histrionics."

She jumped to her feet and stalked down the length of the table with the board members' heads all turning to follow her. "Histrionics?" she spat, as she pointed her finger into his chest.

"This board does not have time for your trivial pursuits, Alessandra," he countered, looking down to take in her brown eyes lit with the fire of her anger.

"Nor your inept attempts at trying to capture the queen in a chess game you're not fully equipped to play," she said coldly.

Alek reached up and lightly captured the finger she pressed into his chest into his hand. "When it comes to business, you're no queen, my dear," he said, his voice low in the small space between them as he instinctively stroked her soft palm with his thumb.

His eyes squinted in surprise when he thought he felt her shiver.

She snatched away from his grip and stepped back from him. “Then why are you so intimidated by me?”

Alek threw his head back and laughed wholeheartedly. “Me? You? Intimidated?” he said in between chuckles.

“Enough!” Aldrich said, jumping to his feet.

Alek and Alessandra looked to the older man, his thin lips still quivering in frustration and his face now reddish with annoyance.

“Do you think your fathers would be proud of your behavior?” he asked, his English accent clipped.

“Yes,” Alessandra answered unequivocally. “Yes, I do.”

Alek looked disbelieving.

“My father wanted me in *this* position. He believed I could handle *this* position. And I have proven—even at the detriment of my own personal happiness—that I can thrive in *this* position,” she said, stalking back to her seat. “And so, if it means standing up for myself to this archaic-minded jackass and his chauvinistic mindset then, yes, I believe my father is in heaven not only standing up and applauding, but wishing he could interject and give some more of the same.”

Alek’s eyes darted to the up-and-down motion of her breasts as she deeply breathed through her anger at him. His desire stirred. This woman who defied him with such fire and authority was not the mousy little Alessandra of the past. This was a different woman. And he wanted her with an intensity that surprised him. He bit back a smile as he calmly unbuttoned his blazer and reclaimed his seat.

Aldrich gave them both stern looks as he took his seat. He had been with the conglomerate since the early days and both thought of him as a family friend. It was respect for him, his position with the company and his friendship with their fathers that stopped the sparks flying between them.

"Do you both have companies in mind set up for an acquisition to become a subsidiary of ADG?" another of the board members asked.

"Yes. My team and I have been narrowing the field for the past couple of months in preparation for this being my first major act as co-CEO. As shown in the reports I gave you all, we have a strong contender," Alessandra said.

"Alek?"

"Yes."

"Liar," she mouthed at him.

*That tongue on the dip of her bottom lip thing is really hot.*

"I believe it would only be viable to explore *one* of these suggestions at this time," Aldrich said, looking from Alessandra to Alek. "The majority vote of the members of this board would constitute the breaking of a…tie."

Alek's and Alessandra's eyes locked across the distance.

He blinked and looked away from her. A craving to kiss her wouldn't release him.

Aldrich cleared his throat. "I suggest you both present your full proposals at next month's meeting and we will hold a vote to settle the matter once and for all."

His fellow board members gave approving nods.

"Fine," Alessandra said, picking up her pen to rotate it between her slender fingers.

Alek remained silent. He was stunned the board was even open to her proposal. And in truth, during her presentation they had been attentive. Respectful, even. *It's time to get more acquainted with Miss Dalmount.*

Over the rim of round, bright red spectacles, the board's secretary, Iris Dennis, eyed the board members from her seat next to Aldrich. "Shall we move on? The meeting does coincide with the thirtieth Jubilee celebration next month to be held at the Lake House. The meeting will be that Thursday and we have confirmed use of a conference room on-site. I would like to quickly review the final preparations for the events that weekend."

Alek tilted his head in acquiescence to Iris as he continued to watch Alessandra closely and find that he liked the look of her. She was stunning. Sophisticated and polished. Poised. She had this subtle sexy that was understated and made a man want to see more. *He* wanted more.

"I would like to make a formal offer to buy you out, Alessandra."

Long after the board meeting had ended and the members had left the conference room, Alek and Alessandra remained in their seats at opposing ends of the table. Moments ticked by and silence reigned.

Alessandra took him in. His low-cut hair, his handsome face, and the broadness of his shoulders in his tailored suit that he wore with such ease that she was sure he owned a hundred or more of them. Physically, everything about him intrigued her. *Traitor.*

"It's time you realize that there is a woman—a qualified woman—sitting at the table in the boys' club, Alek," she finally said, tapping the tip of her nail against the top of the polished wood conference table. "No more running to London to hide from the truth."

*Tap-tap-tap.*

"And do you like being in the company of men, Alessandra, pretending to be one of the boys?" he asked.

Alessandra arched a brow. "Are you questioning my femininity, Alek?" she asked, her voice soft but with an underlying steely edge.

He shook his head and turned his lips downward. "No, of course not," he said, rapping his strong knuckles against the table. "Femininity has nothing to do with sexuality."

Alessandra sighed and leaned back in her chair as she tilted her head to the side to look at him. "Perhaps having women with more looks than intellect fawning over you has distorted your idea of women and what we want, Alek. But please let's be clear that, although I completely understand why a woman would want to be rid of men in every way, including sexually, I am not a lesbian."

"You're not?" he asked in feigned surprise.

She rolled her eyes. "Surprise, surprise, Mr. I Can't Keep My Personal Life Out of the Tabloids. Not every straight woman flings herself at your feet. Some of us have more discretion—and taste."

Alek leaned back in his chair and rubbed his chin. "Perhaps if you stopped playing businesswoman and focused on finding a life of your own, you wouldn't have time to watch mine."

Alessandra fought hard to keep her composure.

Gone was her nervousness, replaced by the fire and indignation his attitude evoked. She enjoyed their banter. She even felt rallied by his challenge. "And perhaps your life entails such a long string of women because you're incapable of satisfying one well enough to stay around," she said, and then offered him a tip of her head. *So there.*

Alessandra rose and gathered her files and folders before turning to walk to the door without another look at him.

"Perhaps if you were my type I would show you how well equipped I am at satisfying a woman."

She froze just as her hand closed around the cool brass of the doorknob. She released a short breath as if a pressure valve had been briefly turned. Allowing herself a five count, she turned and walked the length of the spacious conference room to stand before him. She reached down to grip the back of his chair, bringing their faces just inches apart. His face within a lick of her oxblood-tinted lips, she said, "Physically I am your type, Alek. I am very much your type…and you know it. Humph, it's only my brain and my backbone that you think are a turnoff."

His face was a mask of boredom, but his eyes dipped down to her mouth, and Alessandra saw it. Her breath caught and she rose, backing away from him at the truth of her words in his eyes. She knew desire when she saw it. She turned and quick-walked to the door, trying to hide how much he flustered her.

*"Qui s'enfuit maintenant?"* he asked smoothly in French.

He must have known she spoke it fluently. "Who's running away now?" he'd asked.

*Me. I'm running. Running fast and hard and not stopping one damn bit.*

Alessandra didn't stop her hurried steps until she had left the room and pulled the door closed behind her. With her heart beating rapidly, she licked the dryness from her mouth and allowed herself a moment to press her back to the door as she fought hard to reclaim the coolness she had become known for in the last five years.

Making a pained face, she raised her free hand to lightly knock her wrist against her forehead. "Stupid, stupid, stupid," she admonished herself in a whisper.

The man was a chauvinist who made it clear he wanted her out of the company in which they equally owned the majority of shares. He had no respect for her. No desire to work with her or even be around her.

The doorknob turned against her buttocks a moment before it was opened from behind her. Alessandra's face filled with alarm as she felt her body free-fall backward.

She felt Alek's large hands wrap around her upper arms. The thin material of her shirt did nothing to protect her from the warmth of his touch as he kept her from hitting the floor. Her head landed on one of his shoulders and her back pressed lightly against his chest.

Alessandra felt nothing but strength.

Quickly she turned, accidentally pressing her body back against the open door. "Th-thank—thank you," she stuttered, her nerves completely undone by him.

He stepped up close to her.

Alessandra tried to back away more but there

was nothing but the unrelenting pressure of the door against her back.

"You're welcome, Alessandra," he said softly, before reaching up to lightly stroke her cheek and then her chin before he walked away from her.

She closed her eyes and released a long shaky breath, left with nothing but the warm scent of his cologne and the lingering aftereffects of his touch.

*I wanted to kiss her.*

Alek looked back over his shoulder as he walked down the length of the hall leading to his office. He stopped and turned as Alessandra closed the door to the conference room, pressed her files to her chest and then walked across the reception area. His eyes shifted down to the gentle sway of her hips and buttocks in her pants.

Alek considered himself a connoisseur of woman, and Alessandra Dalmount was top-shelf.

*Very nice*, he thought, not turning away to continue down the hall until she was out of his line of vision.

He walked through the open glass double doors into his outer office.

"Hello, Ms. Kingsley," he said to the woman whose very appearance was the essence of propriety and no-nonsense.

He wanted it that way. He'd experienced the debacle of a young, sexy secretary with her eye on the wealthy executive. He didn't need the temptation.

Ms. Kingsley gave him a smile that didn't reach her cobalt blue eyes. "I entered all your messages on the online log," she said.

Alek patted the inner pocket over his heart where

his iPhone sat. "I got the notifications. Thank you," he said, moving past her desk to open one of the double doors leading into his office.

"Please get Naim Ansah on the line."

"Of course, sir."

With an approving nod, he closed the door and tossed his briefcase on the leather sofa of his reception area before he unbuttoned his silk-lined blazer to remove it and place it on the hanger of the wooden valet standing just outside his private bathroom. Taking his seat behind his massive desk, he signed on to his iPad to check the log of his incoming messages. A few business calls, and at least one message each from his mother, LuLu, his sister, Samira, and his brother, Naim.

He smiled. His return to New York meant more time spent with the family he had left behind five years ago. They visited him often in London, but he was pleased to be back among them regularly. He was sure his mother was already preparing his favorite Ghanaian dish of yam *fufu* and *nkatenkwan*. He couldn't wait to pull off a piece of the *fufu* ball and dip into the stew of chicken cooked in a rich peanut butter sauce and tomatoes with spices.

His stomach grumbled, but he focused on work instead. It was time to get serious about his plan to shift ADG into commercial aviation, and his younger brother was just the help he needed. Naim was younger than him by five years, but he was ambitiously climbing through the ranks of the company through sheer hard work. Nepotism had gotten him in the door but Naim was out to prove that he deserved his seat at the table. In the three years since he had begun at ADG, he had moved up the ranks from a management trainee to a lead position in the marketing division.

*Bzzz.*

"Yes?" he said, continuing to scan the message log.

"Mr. Ansah is in a meeting. Would you like me to continue holding?" Ms. Kingsley asked via the intercom.

Alek held his finger above the tablet at the sight of his ex-wife's name. *Kenzay called?* His brows dipped as he frowned deeply.

"Sir?" Ms. Kingsley gently nudged.

"No. I'll see him later," he said before turning off the intercom.

He leaned back in his chair and swiveled to look out the twenty-foot windows. The warmth of the sunlight framed him as he looked off in the distance at the varying shapes, colors and designs of the neighboring high-rise buildings. *Is Kenzay in New York?*

Usually they reached out to each other only during those rare occasions they were in the same city.

He'd met the beautiful socialite on the elevator of the Burj Al Arab in Dubai. He'd been staying at the hotel while in the country checking on one of ADG's numerous oil refineries; she was on a massive shopping spree sponsored by her father, a real estate developer of luxury hotels and mansions. Within hours they were making love against the floor-to-ceiling windows of his presidential suite with the sapphire ocean as their backdrop. Six months later they were married in a five-million-dollar destination wedding in the Maldives. The honeymoon period came and went quickly. Although their nights were filled with hot sex, their days were nothing but bitter arguments and long stretches of cold silence. They agreed neither wanted to be married and they never truly loved each other. By their second wedding anniversary their divorce was finalized.

Over the last three years, they'd occasionally given in to the attraction that still simmered between them. Neither wanted to reunite permanently and both frequently dated other people. Kenzay's dating life was just as adventurous and well chronicled by the press as his own as she traveled the world on her father's dime and the generous divorce settlement he paid to her based on their prenuptial agreement.

If she was calling she was somewhere nearby. *Maybe an afternoon romp would relax me...*

He picked up the phone to dial her cell phone number but changed his mind with a shake of his head and a downturn of his lips. He didn't have time for the distraction of his ex-wife. He had to stay focused on another woman in his life.

Alek swiveled away from the window. His dark eyes landed on his briefcase on the leather sofa. The file containing Alessandra's proposal was in it. She surprised him with more than just her change in looks and demeanor. She was further ahead on her proposal than he thought.

He swore, leaning back in his leather executive chair and tenting his fingers beneath his strong chin.

Their stalemate in that boardroom was one of the prime reasons he didn't want to share ownership with Alessandra. He wasn't quite sure how their fathers had accomplished it for thirty years. *Because they had been equals. They'd respected each other.*

It was going to take more than an MBA and a makeover for it to sit well that he was forced to share the company and the decision-making with Alessandra Dalmount. For years, she'd shown not one modicum of business savvy and suddenly she was a savant? He refused to swallow that.

Alek jumped up from his chair, causing to it to roll back and softly hit against the glass as he made his way across the expansive office. He snatched up his briefcase and pulled out his copy of her proposal. *Why can't she just go away quietly?*

His hand crumpled the corner inside his fist before he flung it down onto the couch.

*And why can't I stop wondering how her mouth would taste?*

"Damn," he swore.

*"Physically I am your type, Alek. I am very much your type...and you know it. Humph, it's only my brain and my backbone that you think are a turnoff."*

She was almost right on that point.

He did want her...but he wanted her out of his business affairs more.

They were a month from celebrating the thirtieth anniversary of the conglomerate his father and Alessandra's father had formed. Thirty years rich with a history that had to be protected and preserved. He respected the brilliance of Frances Dalmount, but his choice to make his daughter his heir had been made with his heart and not the cunning intellect he was well respected for.

Alek was intent on correcting the error.

He would rather have Alessandra Dalmount in his bedroom than his boardroom.

*Perhaps I can kill two birds with one stone.*

For one moment, one *very* brief moment, he allowed himself to imagine wooing Alessandra so much that she gave up any foolish notions of being a businesswoman. His conscience won out. He was a businessman and not a man-whore using his wares to convince women to do as he pleased.

Alessandra didn't deserve to be his partner, but she definitely didn't deserve to have her heart and body toyed with, either.

Alek sat down on the sofa and pulled the conference phone closer to press the intercom button. "Ms. Kingsley."

"Sir?"

"I need to speak with each of the board members, starting with Aldrich Brent," he said. "Call each one. Give me thirty minutes and get the next on the line."

"Yes, sir."

He rubbed his hands together in the moments before his phone buzzed. It was time to gauge just what side the board was going to choose. He couldn't do anything about her ownership, but he could call for a vote for her to be officially removed as chief executive officer.

# *Chapter 3*

*Three weeks later*

Alessandra closed her copies of the *Wall Street Journal* and *New York Times* and picked up her cup of lavender tea to take several deep sips before she sat it down and reached for her iPad. Enjoying the feel of the July sun blazing through the windows of her two-story penthouse apartment, she connected with the online editions of *International Business Times*, London's *Financial Times* and Italy's *Corriere della Sera*. All five newspapers were a part of her normal routine, but she preferred the feel of the print paper against her fingers as she turned the pages.

Just like her beloved books. She was still a voracious reader of those set during the Elizabethan era and had curated a small collection of rare first editions of authors of that era. There was something to be said for tradition. Respect for the past.

"You have an old soul, my Alessandra," her father would say, and then playfully pinch her nose.

She smiled at the memory as she looked around at the French country design of her luxurious apartment with its soft muted tones, high-end furnishings, fine art and sweeping views of the Manhattan skyline. She grew up surrounded by such excess, but she had never felt at ease. Her style was simplistic. It was a part of her inheritance from her father, and she could never imagine changing the decor or getting rid of the apartment. It was just as her father had left it and he'd had it designed in the taste her mother would have loved. And so, for all its grandeur, living in the penthouse made her feel closer to them both.

Alessandra looked down the length of the table large enough to seat twelve people. Every empty chair was a reminder of her loneliness. Her longing caused an ache to radiate across her chest.

She didn't long for more people in her life. She wasn't even interested in dating with her focus on her career. No, Alessandra just wanted less space to echo around her.

The penthouse was a place to stay during the week while she was in Manhattan. Home was the family estate in Passion Grove, New Jersey. She smiled. Passion Grove. She absolutely loved the small town and couldn't wait to get there on Friday evenings.

Although the vast majority of the residents were wealthy, the town was ideal for those with luxurious homes still wanting to enjoy the small-town feel. Everyone knew one another and there were many events and holidays the townspeople enjoyed together. For her, Passion Grove, with its heart-shaped lake and streets named after flowers, was ideal.

Alessandra looked up as her maid silently entered the room to begin clearing her dishes. "Tell Cook everything was delicious as always, Gia," she said before rising from the table, setting her linen napkin atop her nearly empty plate.

Gia nodded. "I will," she said warmly. "Have a good day, Ms. Dalmount."

"Same to you, Gia," she said, offering her a soft smile. "Thanks."

Alessandra was well aware her demeanor with her staff at her various homes was different than with her staff at work. She had nothing to prove at home. No one was judging her. She could be herself, and that was thoughtful and kind. At ADG, that would be taken for weakness.

She chuckled as she used a crimson-red stiletto-shaped nail to ease her hair back behind her ear. "Elsa," she said with another chuckle. The modern take on calling her the ice queen. Alessandra mockingly pretended to pout at the memory. When she discovered that's what she was called behind her back, the last thing she did was "let it go." Instead she took the chill factor up a notch. "I gave them frozen, all right."

Her footsteps echoed against the travertine stone floors. The reminder of the emptiness of the five-bedroom apartment was deafening. She passed the door leading into her father's palatial master suite and her own childhood bedroom still decorated in shades of baby pink and ivory with an abundance of ruffles. She had long ago selected the largest of the three guest suites, preferring the more adult decor.

She removed the white floor-length robe she wore, already missing the cool feel of the woven cotton as she lay it across the foot of the king-size upholstered bed. In the walk-in closet separating the bedroom from the en suite spa bathroom hung a row of clear garment bags. Thirty in all. Each was labeled with a date with a clear shoe container on the shelf above it.

This was the playland of her stylist, Shiva Delacroix. Alessandra just visited it daily to wear whatever ensemble Shiva had prepared for that day. Everything from undergarments to accessories were readied, making her mornings easy and sending her into corporate America ready for war as if her clothing were her armor.

Another facade.

Alessandra turned the first bag and unzipped it to remove a burnt-orange button-up blouse teamed with flared trousers with racing stripes. She tore the Polaroid photo from the bag and set it atop the island in the center of the room, before removing the clothing from the suede hangers and getting dressed. She hummed Beyoncé's "Grown Woman" as she checked the correct fit of the clothing by the model in the photo.

She undid the buttons exposing the top of her cleavage, pushed up the sleeves to her elbows, and made sure the multi-strand gold chain she wore just barely peeked from beneath the shirt. She rushed through slipping on the leopard-print calf-hair pumps and her favorite Patek Philippe watch and grabbing the clutch Shiva selected before leaving her suite.

In the foyer, she picked up her briefcase and keys

from the table as she checked her watch and left the apartment through her private entrance and elevator. It opened into the first level of her exclusive parking area.

*Ding.*

The doors slid open and as expected her driver, Roje, was already waiting outside her father's black 1954 Jaguar MK VII sedan. As a little girl, she could remember standing on the porch of their mansion in Passion Grove as her dad climbed into the back and was driven to work each day. Ever since her first day of work at ADG she had used the car, as well. It felt like a full circle moment.

With a soft smile to the tall and burly man of sixty with skin as dark and smooth as midnight and a bright white goatee, she slid inside, setting her purse on the leather seat beside her. Roje was her bodyguard and her driver. She held no fear in his presence. His name was of his Jamaican heritage and meant "a person who is a guard." It suited him perfectly.

"Shiva's showroom, Roje," she requested, as she let her head fall back on the seat. Her eyes drifted closed.

She wasn't physically tired, just weary at the thought of yet another fitting.

Thursday would see the start of the extended weekend-long celebration to mark the company's thirtieth Jubilee anniversary. It was to be held at one of ADG's properties, the Lake House, a castle resort in upstate New York. Luncheons, picnics, art exhibits, tours, bike rides, boating, rock climbing and a charity tennis game were on the schedule. All the high-ranking executives and their families were invited, along with business colleagues and the press. The weekend would culminate in a lavish ball to officially welcome Alessandra and Alek to their positions.

She was headed into Midtown Manhattan for the final fitting of her couture Zuhair Murad gown. Alessandra turned her head on the rest to look out the tinted window at the abundance of skyscrapers and hotels as Roje maneuvered the traffic on FDR Drive. The distance between Shiva's showroom and the ADG offices was less than ten miles, but the drive would undoubtedly take every bit of twenty-five minutes.

She'd barely carved out the time for Shiva, because her focus had been on her report for the board. Their meeting was tomorrow morning at the Lake House before the celebratory festivities were scheduled to begin. Their vote of approval was the last step to ADG's purchasing the controlling shares in ZiCorp, the shipping company she had personally selected and vetted for acquisition. It would serve as the perfect opportunity for ADG to branch into Greece, with personnel and an established customer base in place. She and her team had addressed every possible issue that might arise and any concern the board could have. Months of arduous work would hopefully pay off. The company was in solid shape and would be nothing but an asset to ADG, with a return on the purchase price of controlling shares of ZiCorp projected to be recouped within a year.

During her training time at ADG Alessandra had chosen to focus on mergers and acquisitions, particularly in the areas of favorable purchase price, market movement and successful integration techniques. This was the first deal she had managed, but it was solid.

She wanted to beat Alek. To humble him. To prove him wrong.

To earn his respect.

*No.* She purposefully pushed any thought of him aside, closing her eyes and shaking her head a bit to free her mind of any thought of the handsome—yet infuriating—rogue. He took up enough time in her life antagonizing her during the day and invading her dreams with wild thoughts at night.

"Ms. Dalmount."

Alessandra opened her eyes. They were double-parked on Seventh Avenue outside the eighteen-story building where Shiva had set up a showroom for her impressive roster of clients. Usually, Shiva would come to her for measurements or fittings, but on occasion Alessandra preferred the normalcy of going to the showroom.

Roje now stood with the rear door open and his hand already outstretched to her. Picking up her purse, she accepted his assistance as she stepped onto the street. "Thank you," she said, easing through the pedestrians, tourists and locals alike, who moved up and down the street with speed. "I shouldn't be more than an hour, Roje."

"Yes, ma'am," he said, stepping ahead of her to open the glass door leading into the beautifully tiled lobby.

Alessandra rode one of the four elevators of the beautiful office building to the third floor. Through the glass wall and the double doors of the entrance to Shiva's showroom, she took in the two thousand square feet of loft-style space lined with clothing racks and adorned mannequins with bright light streaming in from the windows.

She smiled and waved at Shiva, who was looking on as one of her three assistants adjusted the hem of an emerald satin strapless gown on a woman standing before a wall of mirrors.

"I'll be right with you, Alessandra," Shiva said, kneeling to lift the hem and then release it.

The woman before the mirror turned to look over her shoulder. She was a tall, caramel-skinned beauty with shoulder-length auburn hair and hazel eyes. She smiled at her as if they knew each other.

They did not.

Alessandra sat her clutch on the low-slung white leather couch running along the glass wall as she eyed her. The woman was stunning, and that would be a fact in or out of her beautiful formfitting dress.

"I see Shiva will be styling us both for the ball," she said with a friendly grin and an accent that was English.

Alessandra stiffened and offered her a cool smile. "And you are?" she asked politely

"Millicent… Alek's date for the weekend," she answered smoothly.

Alessandra fought not to frown. *A date? He would.*

"See you tomorrow then," she said, deliberately softening her tone because it wasn't the woman's fault Alek was a philanderer who couldn't stand to attend an event without arm candy.

"Okay, Milli, you're all set," Shiva said, raking her fingers through her waist-length jet-black hair. "If you go get changed, we'll package the dress for you to take with you."

Millicent smiled and showed perfect teeth before she lifted the dress and carefully walked to the rear of the showroom to the curtained-off dressing room area. The woman looked like Jessica Rabbit.

"You're welcome," Shiva said, as she strolled up to Alessandra in a floor-length white tunic and army boots.

"For my dress, yes, thank you as always, Shiva," Alessandra said, her tone distracted as she drew her iPhone from her clutch and pulled up her contact list.

Shiva pressed her hand down against the screen.

She looked up in surprise at the thirtysomething Cuban woman with striking features that made her an odd beauty.

"I scheduled your fittings like this on purpose," Shiva said, waving at her male assistant, who pushed a body form covered with white silk.

Alessandra swiped Shiva's hand from her phone and scrolled through the list with the steady stroke of her thumb against the screen. *There is no way I am attending the ball alone now. No. Way. In. Hell.*

"Bring it to me but do not uncover it just yet," Shiva called across the busy showroom.

"Hill," Alessandra said, thinking of the corporate attorney she'd had lunch with weeks ago. He was boyishly handsome, well-dressed and successful. They had no chemistry, but he would suffice for the night. *Wait...would that mean I'm using him?*

Shiva gently removed her phone.

Alessandra frowned. Over the years they had become good friends and not just stylist and client.

"I wanted you to see Alek's date in her dress," she

explained with a wink. "And give you a chance to wear the dress I *first* suggested."

The two women shared a look before Alessandra adamantly shook her head, causing her hair to move back and forth against her nape.

Millicent walked up to them with her garment bag hung carefully over her arm. She looked just as striking in a simple white T and distressed boyfriend jeans with heels. "Bye, Shiva. And nice meeting you, Alessandra," she said before leaving the showroom with long, model-like strides.

"You know the good thing about having that custom body form made to your specifications is that I really didn't need you to fit the new dress to your body, *mi amiga Inocente*," she said.

Alessandra spoke Spanish, as well. "Yes, I'm your friend but I am *not* innocent," she said defensively, looking toward the silk-covered form being rolled toward them.

"Humph," Shiva teased, accepting the black garb a petite pink-haired assistant handed her.

She held it in front of Alessandra's body as she steered her toward the wall of mirrors. The lace dress with long sheer sleeves and flowing A-line skirt was covered with delicate floral designed beadwork.

"This is exquisite. Beautiful and classic," Shiva emphasized. "But *that* one will make sure you are the queen of the ball…"

Alessandra looked over as the white silk drape was snatched with dramatic flair from the body form. She gasped a bit as the light from the window seemed to shine like a spotlight on the gown. The moment was very cliché, but also very fitting. The dress was amazing. "It's not…*too* much?" she asked in a whisper, like a child in a library trying not to get caught talking.

"It's *just* enough," Shiva said, her voice a whisper, as well.

Alessandra stepped from behind the black frock Shiva held to stand before the dress form.

"Millicent who?" Shiva asked.

Alessandra looked over her shoulder to give her a look, like, "Really, Shiva?"

The woman shrugged.

"I'll try it on," Alessandra said, heading back to one of the dressing rooms.

"Yes! Take that, Alek Ansah!" Shiva exclaimed in victory, well aware of Alessandra's rocky relationship with the man.

*Maybe it's time for the ice queen to serve up a little heat.*

Alessandra was anxious to get to the office. Shiva was having the dress delivered to the Lake House in the morning. It was time to get refocused on work. The final printed proposals were to be on her desk before she walked through the door. She had no doubt that they were.

"The side entrance, Roje," she requested, her eyes looking out the window at the busy New York traffic.

"Yes, ma'am," he said, his voice rough and his Jamaican accent clear.

He drove the vintage Jaguar down the one-way street and parked outside the art deco building that spoke to its creation in the 1930s. She tucked her clutch under her arm and slid on her shades as he left the car and came around to open the rear door for her. Sliding her hand inside the one he offered, she stepped onto the street. She wasn't in the mood to speak to anyone, and the private entrance was ideal. On the opposite side of the building, Alek had his own, as well.

She paused to look up at the bright sunlight breaking through the tall buildings. For a moment, she just enjoyed the feel of the sun and thought back to a simpler time when she would lie by the pool and read literary classics when she wasn't doing volunteer work for one of her many humanitarian efforts.

Her smile was melancholy as she turned and entered the pass code to the nondescript-looking door. The shadow of Roje's large body behind her was comforting as he reached around her to open the door to a narrow and short hall leading directly to a private elevator that only stopped on the penthouse floor. She hardly used this entrance, preferring the massive and elaborate entrance into the front lobby.

The well-worn black-and-white checkerboard tile and the ornate wrought iron door to the elevator spoke to its originality to the building. Although the security features had been updated, nothing else had been touched.

The outer door closed behind them and locked as she pressed her thumb to the fingerprint reader. The lock echoed in the small space.

*Clank.*

"Have a good day, Ms. Dalmount," Roje said, opening the wrought iron gate.

Alessandra stepped inside and removed her shades, tucking them inside her purse. "Same to you, Roje."

With a nod, he turned and exited. Just as the elevator began to ascend, she watched on the security monitor in the corner as he climbed into the vehicle and pulled away, leaving the street empty.

She allowed a break in her usual cool demeanor as she fidgeted anxiously and fought the urge to press the button again for the top level of the building as if that would speed its journey there. “Relax, Alex,” she said, reverting to her childhood nickname.

The elevator came to a stop and opened into the hall just outside her terrace entrance. She barely spared the elegant and spacious outdoor setting a glance as she made her way across the large expanse. Her footsteps echoed her quick pace to reach her desk.

She dropped her briefcase and purse on her desk as she eyed the stack of leather folders. She immediately picked one up and sat down in her chair to pore over every word, photo and graph on every page. She hardly noticed when she heard Unger arrive to work and begin his day. Soon, he quietly entered and sat a cup of lemon tea on her desk. At home, the lavender relaxed her before a full day of work, and at the office the lemon invigorated her.

He knew her routine well.

Taking a sip of her tea, she gave the pitch a careful final perusal for error. She refused to let a typo or an error by the printer ruin her presentation to the board. Alessandra nodded her head in approval as she closed the folder and then settled back in her chair. She was ready for her presentation to the board in the morning. *Is he?*

Alessandra rose from her seat and walked over to the glass-front wine cooler to remove a bottle of 1995 Krug Clos d’Ambonnay champagne and grabbed two flutes from her bar. She tucked one of the proposal packets under her arm.

She walked behind her desk to the shelves of books lining the wall. With a gentle push against the shelf to the far right, it swung open, revealing a long, windowless concrete hallway that ran along the back wall of the boardroom and connected to Alek's office on the other end. Another of the secrets the building held.

Her father had shown it to her ages ago when she was six or seven.

It was her first time using it. Would Alek be shocked by it? Alessandra shrugged. "Well, let's see," she said.

Her heels clicked against the dull concrete, echoing against the unadorned walls, as she reached the other end.

She was surprised when the door opened suddenly and his presence filled the doorway. She felt slightly flustered at the sight of him sans jacket with his sleeves rolled up and his tie loosened.

He motioned with his hand for her to enter before turning to walk back into his office.

"I've been summoned," she whispered as she followed him, disappointed that she couldn't surprise him.

In the three weeks since they moved offices she'd never ventured into his space before. The similarities were clear, although his had more of a masculine and modern edge. As he continued on his call she looked down at the framed photos on the edge of his massive desk. She recognized his mother and siblings. *Um, Naim and Samira.*

The entire family was beautiful, brown and bold.

"Let me call you back. I have a…visitor," Alek said before swiftly hitting a button on his phone and then removing his earbud.

Alessandra set the champagne and flutes on a clear spot on his desk. "Video surveillance, Alek? Really?" she asked, spotting the digital images on his iPad. "Thank goodness I didn't sneak a nose pick."

"It's your nose, Alessandra," he said, shifting his weight in the chair before leaning back and smoothing his hand over his beard as he watched her with those dark eyes.

Her heartbeat went awry under his watchful gaze. "I thought we should celebrate," she said, lightly tapping the cork on the bottle.

Alek gave her a once-over before leaning forward to take it from her.

She instantly felt warmed by the slight touch of his fingers against her hand. "This weekend we celebrate thirty years of ADG and our official claim to the thrones of the empire our fathers created together," she said, discreetly wiping her hand against her thigh as if she could erase the slight tingle that remained from his touch.

Alek opened the rare bottle with ease and filled each of the flutes slowly.

"Even *if* you've made it clear you don't think I deserve it just as much as you just because I use the facilities sitting down instead of standing up," she said smoothly before accepting the flute he handed her.

He chuckled. "To the Ansah Dalmount Group," he said, holding his drink out to her.

Alessandra arched a brow and lightly touched her

flute to his before taking a deep sip. "And to the completion of a comprehensive report that will seal the Zi-Corp deal tomorrow. *Salute*."

Alek fell just short of taking a sip as he paused the flute and eyed her over the rim. "I'm going to hate to see such a beautiful woman filled with disappointment," he said before finally allowing himself a large gulp of the smooth champagne that was well worth the four-figure price tag.

"My beauty is of no relevance to this conversation," she said, moving to sit on the edge of his desk.

"Of no relevance but very hard to deny," Alek said in a low voice, rising from his seat to come around and lean against the desk beside her. His shoulder brushed against hers.

Alessandra's heart fluttered as if filled with the wings of a million butterflies.

"I'm not equipped to handle all this...flattery, Alek," she began, giving him a side-eye as she subtly shifted her body to place a few inches between them. "I left my boots at home."

He eased his body over to close the gap she created. The warmth of his body and his cologne were overwhelming. *Why did I come in here to play with fire?*

Her awareness of Alek Ansah wasn't diminishing. Being in his presence made her senses go on alert. And the fact that he seemed as unable to hide his desire for her as he was his antagonism was its own kind of torture.

She stood up and tilted her head back to finish off the champagne before she turned and walked to the hidden door. His mocking and all too telling chuckle followed by her. Aware that his eyes were on her, she measured her steps because she didn't want it to appear that she was running again…even though she was.

*"Non abbiate paura di ottenere una regina calda e bella del ghiaccio."*

She paused at his words spoken fluently in Italian. She thought of the gown she would wear to the ball and if that would prove that the ice queen was not afraid to get hot. "Just how many languages do you speak, Alek?" she asked over her shoulder.

"Five," he answered. "But I will only speak to you in one of the four you speak, Alessandra."

She turned, her hand lightly grasping the edge of the portal. "And how many does Millicent speak?" she asked.

His handsome face filled with the surprise she sought earlier.

Alessandra held up her hand when he began to speak. "Don't answer that. I'm sure when you two are together she doesn't speak because her mouth is full," she said slyly.

Alek laughed. Loud and boisterous, with his head flung back and his beautiful mouth opened wide. He clapped. "Good one, Alessandra. Very good one. You're very quick on your feet."

"Goodbye, Alek," she said.

"And you're jealous," he added.

*Yes. I am.*

She walked back over to where he still leaned against the edge of his desk to stand before him. With a lick of her glossed lips, she reached for his tie and gently wrapped the ends around her fist to tug him forward until their faces were inches apart.

Their eyes locked.

Their breaths mingled in that small air between their mouths.

That primal awareness between them pulsed with life.

His eyes dipped to take in her pouty mouth before rising back to her eyes. She saw the heat of desire in the ebony depths.

"I am jealous of the one thing I can't seem to get from you," she whispered, her words pressing against his hungry mouth. "And that's your *respect*."

His face filled with shock. "Huh?"

It was Alessandra's turn to chuckle as she released his silk tie and smoothed it against his chest.

*Oh my God. I can feel his muscles.*

She suppressed her urge to roughly tear his custom shirt open and press her hands greedily to his abdomen. "Goodbye and good luck tomorrow, Alek," she said, quickly moving away from him.

He reached out and grabbed her wrist. His touch was electrifying.

She shivered, trying in vain to tug free of his strong hold.

And then suddenly he released her and stood to move past her, tipping his head back to finish the rest of his champagne. "Leave, Alessandra," he said, his voice tight with anger. "Get out."

Alessandra hurried out of his office through the secret passageway, surprised by his anger. She had barely taken two steps into the hall when the door closed and the turn of the lock echoed around her. She looked back and then up until she spotted the small camera in the corner.

Her face was stoic as she turned and walked the length of the hall with measured steps until she, too, was behind her closed and locked hidden door.

## Chapter 4

Alek was still haunted by that moment in his office with Alessandra earlier that day. Not even his attendance at a luxurious dinner party hosted by his best friend, Chance Castillo, at his estate in Alpine, New Jersey, could free him of the hot memory. Her taunt had angered him because he fell for it. In that moment with nothing but space and opportunity between them, he had wanted to feel the softness of her mouth on his own. He didn't want to hunger for Alessandra, but he did. At odd moments of the day he imagined just how he would stoke the same fire from her in passion as he did in anger. During meetings, she would distract him with the smell of her perfume or the cut of her clothing on her curvaceous body. At night, when he tried to rest she was there in his dreams, causing him to awaken with an aching erection like a virginal schoolboy.

He wanted Alessandra Dalmount. Badly. In a rushed, hot, *rip your clothes off and fill her with every hard inch you got while up against the wall* kind of way.

He swore into his snifter of Grand Marnier Cuvée 1880.

"Something wrong, stranger?"

Alek looked up from where he sat on the bench of a nine-foot Brazilian rosewood Steinway grand piano to find his ex-wife, Kenzay. She wore a white lace romper that exposed the silk bralette and panty beneath it. The color looked fabulous against her deep brown complexion and highlighted her long, shapely legs. During their marriage, they would have argued about such a revealing outfit, but now he just enjoyed the show.

Rising to his feet, he grabbed her waist to pull her close for a hug. "Hello, stranger," he whispered in her ear before planting a warm kiss to her lobe.

She squeezed his elbows. "I called you the last time I was in town," she said. "I needed a fix."

He leaned back from her to look in her eyes. He couldn't help but smile. He knew they shared the memory of hot sex in an elevator when they last saw each other months ago.

"You know what seeing you in a tux does to me," she whispered in his ear.

Yes. Yes, he did.

*Ding-ding-ding.*

The varied conversations of the dinner guests died down as everyone in the music room turned to Chance's butler standing near the entrance of the dining room. "Dinner is served," he said, turning to push open the double doors, exposing a table set for twenty with tall elaborate glass-blown floral arrangements and candle lighting. Chance's taste ran toward vibrant and colorful contemporary style. It was an environment that spoke to his fun-loving personality.

The crowd began to move forward.

Kenzay slid her arm around his.

"Shouldn't you care if I have a date?" Alek asked as they followed the throng.

"Not at all," she assured him.

They made their way into the dining room.

"Alek," Chance said to him from the head of the table, patting the seat to his right.

With Kenzay still attached to him, Alek made his way to his seat. He held the chair next to him for her to slide her tall frame into before he claimed his own.

"Kenzay, I didn't know you were in town," Chance said, spreading his bright red napkin across his lap.

"I just got in today," Kenzay said, reaching under the ebony wood table to massage Alek's inner thigh. "I had to come and get something I wanted."

Alek just shook his head, denying her as he removed her hand, gently setting it back in her own lap. He saw the surprise and anger in her eyes before she masked them.

Kenzay did not like to be denied.

He looked across the table at Chance's girlfriend of the last six months, Helena Guzman. She was a petite, almost waiflike, fair-skinned beauty with waist-length blond hair as bone-straight as her frame. "Have you met Kenzay?" he asked as one of the servers set his plate atop the red square charger before him on the table.

Helena smiled and looked across the table at Kenzay. "Actually, I invited her," she admitted, her Cuban accent very subtle. "We met years ago at boarding school in Switzerland."

Alek and Chance shared a brief look before they both smiled in disbelief.

"Surprise, surprise," Kenzay said, having leaned close to whisper in his ear.

*Ding-ding-ding.*

Alek stopped feasting on the delicious Cuban dinner as his friend and host rose from his seat with his fork and his glass in his hand. The swinging doors leading from the kitchen opened, and the uniformed servers entered the dining room carrying trays of flutes filled with champagne.

"What now, Chance?" Alek asked playfully as he accepted his flute.

Everyone seated around the table laughed or chuckled.

Chance nodded his head in acquiescence. "Well, first I would like to officially welcome my friend—my brother—back to New York. We have all missed your constant presence—and your smart mouth—over the last five years."

Alek smiled and lifted his flute slightly in thanks.

"I am surrounded by friends and family, and I could not think of a better time to share some good news," he said, holding out his free hand to Helena.

She rose to stand beside Chance and captured his hand in the middle of both of hers.

Everyone at the table stirred and murmurs rose.

Chance dropped his head and smiled. "Let me get to it, since I can tell guesses have been made," he said.

"Last week Helena graciously accepted my proposal to become my bride."

Alek's face filled with disbelief even as he rose to hug first his friend and then his fiancée. "Congratulations," he said to them both.

"I can finally wear my ring," Helena said as she drew a chain from the V-neck of her stylish jumpsuit. She pulled it over her head and unclasped the lock to drop the ring into her palm.

Chance picked it up and reached for her left hand. *"Por siempre, mi amor,"* he said, using the language of their shared Cuban heritage as he slid the ring onto her slender finger.

Helena rose up on her toes, pressing her hands to his broad shoulders before kissing his lips.

*Forever, my love.*

Alek frowned at the idea of his friend's words to his fiancée as he gave Chance one last strong pat on the back before moving away from them to allow the waiting guests to congratulate the couple, as well.

Picking up his glass of champagne from his spot at the table, he pressed a kiss to Kenzay's temple and moved to walk through one of the four sets of French doors lining the dining room to step out onto the terrace. As he took a deep sip of champagne he instantly recognized as Dom Pérignon, he inhaled the scent of Sicilian honey lilies heavy in the night air.

In the days before sports and girls had drawn his full-time attention, Alek had spent lots of time with his mother as she tended to her gardens. He knew many a flower by scent alone from those hours. In the days right after his father's tragic death, he had returned to spending time with his mother in her beloved terrace gardens of her apartment on the Upper East Side until she had finally sent him on his way to live life and to let her live hers without a watchdog—albeit a loving one.

Alek smiled. His mother was nothing if not direct.

"Your date looks lonely."

He glanced over his shoulder at Chance stepping out onto the paved terrace, as well.

"Kenzay is not my date, your girl…eh, *fiancée*, invited her," Alek reminded him. "I just needed a moment to let it digest that my friend is getting married."

Chance nodded as he looked out at the stars in the night sky, which was deepening from a cobalt blue to jet-black. "Just like I had to when you married Kenzay," he said with a chuckle.

"Not a good example."

They fell silent.

They were good friends and in many ways closer than Alek was to his own brother. He knew he could fill the silence with warnings of marrying too soon and urgings to make sure she was the one, but he didn't. He couldn't. *Not yet.*

"Are you that surprised? We've been seeing each other for the last six months—and locked it down to just me and her for last three of those months," Chance said, turning to lean back against the metal railing securing the solid glass that gave him unobstructed views of his landscaped garden below.

"And I've been out of the country so I wasn't aware it was that serious," Alek offered. "But I am happy for you."

"Maybe you're next," Chance said, bending to pick

up a stone that he threw across the wildflowers surrounding his villa-style home.

Alek laughed wholeheartedly at that. "Maybe not," he assured him. "I'm still recovering from Kenzay, remember?"

It was Chance's turn to laugh. "There is nothing wrong with having the life your parents had. The love. The kids. The happily-ever-after."

"Yes, but my mother was home full-time," Alek reminded him.

"And my mother worked to provide for me alone," Chance reminded him.

"Wouldn't you prefer she didn't have to work?" Alek asked.

"Of course, *but* it brought her pride that she relied on no one but herself," Chance said. "I never expected Helena to trade being an attorney for being a full-time homemaker, but that's her plan."

Alek gulped his champagne as if it were cheap swill. "Seriously?" he asked, his doubt clear.

Chance nodded with a proud smile. "She surprised me. Helena has always been career driven, but the ring changed all of that, I suppose."

Alek turned and leaned against the low metal railing surrounding the terrace. "What if she changes her mind again?"

"I still want her to be the woman I spend the rest of my life loving."

"Then I am happy for you, my friend," Alek said with honesty.

Alek wasn't looking for a lasting love nor a long-term relationship, but he had often thought of having children of his own. For a man in his position of wealth and prominence, he knew to have one without the other was a risk he wasn't willing to take. Billion-dollar baby mama drama? A straight catastrophe. So the kids would wait until he found the right woman to marry the next time. The only thing he knew for sure was that his wife would be a traditional, stay-at-home mother.

Nothing at all like Alessandra Dalmount.

Alek frowned and shook his head. Thinking of her—even in judgment—

In that moment was an oddity.

Chance looked off into the distance. "Any preliminary votes from the board?"

Alek nodded. "I have three on board. I plan to meet with the others sometime this weekend."

Chance nodded. "So it's working?"

"I just need three more for the majority."

"And?"

"My sources tell me Alessandra hasn't even made an attempt to reach out to the board in the interim," he said, remembering a moment in a recent meeting when she absentmindedly stroked her throat as she listened intently to the president of their casino division. That one innocent move led to a vision of him pressing his mouth to the exact same spot as she stroked his bare back and cried out in pleasure.

"Don't underestimate her, though," Chance reminded him with the hint of a smile at his lips.

The hot image faded as he focused on his friend.

Unlike Alek, Chance came from humble beginnings, raised by a hardworking Afro-Dominican single mother who worked double shifts as a certified nursing assistant to give her lone son the best life she could. When he turned ten she moved them from the Bronx to the Lower East Side, taking on higher rent, to be closer to the fringes of the Upper East Side and fought hard to pay his annual tuition and fees to attend the Dalton School. It was at the elite Manhattan private school that Chance and Alek met and became the best of friends.

His mother, Esmeralda, was more than proud of her son, who went on to finish at Dalton and graduated from Harvard with a degree in accounting and finance. He was a wealthy man in his own right after selling a project management app for well over $600 million. That plus the dividends from smart investing were rocketing him toward billionaire status.

Chance was the epitome of someone using others' underestimation of him for motivation to succeed.

Alek nodded. "Never. She's no idiot."

"And not hard on the eyes," Chance offered.

This time he recalled when Alessandra flipped her hair back over her shoulder and exposed the smooth caramel expanse of her delicate neck. It played like a movie in his mind. He had been filled with a desire to press his lips to her pulse and inhale deeply of the subtle scent of her perfume. He wasn't surprised when he woke up that night from a dream of doing just that and much more to her.

Burying his face against her warm spots. Her cleavage. Her belly. Between her thighs.

Massaging her shoulders.

Teasing her nipples and then sucking them.

Licking a trail from the curve above her buttocks and up her spine.

"The awkward duckling became one hell of a swan," Alek admitted.

"Perhaps you should give her something more to love than just business," Chance joked.

"And who is this?"

Both men turned to find Helena and Kenzay joining them on the terrace.

Helena moved to Chance to massage his back. "We caught the end of your conversation and I need answers, Senor Castillo."

Kenzay took Alek's drink from him and finished it as she eyed him over the gold-trimmed rim.

"I was just telling Alek how you volunteered to put your career on hold once were married," Chance began, wrapping his arm around her waist to pull her body in front of his. She immediately leaned back against him.

"And he joked that was a good way for me to get rid of Alessandra Dalmount," Alek finished.

Helena made a face as she swatted Chance's hand in reprimand. "That's terrible," she said before smiling and kissing his chin.

"Well, speaking as someone who has *experienced* Alek, that is not a good way to get rid of any woman," Kenzay joked with a wink.

Alek took a mock bow.

They all groaned and laughed as they made their way back inside to the party.

For a moment, Alek thought of how much fun wooing and bedding Alessandra could be, but marrying her? Never. She was too firmly entrenched in her role as businesswoman to *ever* satisfy him as wife.

* * *

*"Let me take this off while you watch me..."*

*Alek lay on the middle of the king-size bed. The moonlight cascaded in through the open ten-foot-tall terrace doors. The sultry sound of Beyoncé's song "Rocket" filled the air. A breeze filled with the scent of night-blooming jasmine wafted in, caressing the sheer curtains a bit.*

*He was waiting. And naked.*

*And anxious.*

*He closed his eyes and tilted his head back on the pillow as his Adam's apple rose and fell with his deep swallow. He tugged at the ties on his wrists and ankles that secured him to the four-poster bed.*

*"You ready, Mr. Ansah?"*

*His eyes opened to find Alessandra standing at the foot, her svelte body barely covered by a sheer black lace bodysuit. Her smile was soft and beguiling as she wrapped her hands around his ankles and climbed up onto the bed, her hands inching up to his thighs to massage the defined contours.*

*Her touch was ideal. Soft, barely there, but electrifying.*

*His breath was bated. His pulse soared. And his heart felt right on the edge of a soft explosion.*

*He felt drugged. He was addicted. He wanted—no, needed—more.*

*Desire hardened him until it was thicker and longer. Aching. Needing. Wanting...more.*

*Alessandra dragged her teeth against her bottom lip as she sat back on her knees between his open legs and took him in her hands.*

*He hissed between clenched teeth at the feel of her*

*warm hands on him, stroking him as she brought her thumb up to graze against the smooth tip.*

*"Alessandra," Alek cried out, his hips arching up off the bed.*

*With her eyes locked on him she lowered her head, bowing to him in a way, before she wet her lips with her tongue and then took his hardness into her mouth. Slowly. Inch by inch.*

*Sweat coated his body. His thighs trembled. His gut clenched. His bit his own lip to keep from crying out at the feel of her mouth on him until he felt the tip touch the back of her throat.*

*She swallowed, contracting her throat and causing the base of her tongue to rise up and put sweet pressure on him.*

*Alek whimpered as he felt a small of bit of release jolt in the back of her throat.*

*She moaned in pleasure and swallowed again.*

*"No!" he cried out, straining against the ties with such strength that his entire body bounced up off the bed a bit.*

*She hummed as she slid her mouth up to the tip. She circled it with the tip of her tongue and then sucked it deeply, again and again, as she pressed her tongue against his hard heat.*

*"Please," he begged her, his shame lost amid his abandon.*

*He dwelled somewhere between pleasure and insanity.*

*Alessandra gave one last one kiss to the tip before she freed him.*

*His body relaxed but his heart pounded with a ferocity that frightened him. He closed his eyes and re-*

*leased a long shaky breath. "Damn," he swore in a whisper.*

*His respite was brief. Every muscle making up the hard contours of his body tensed in anticipation as she moved her body to straddle his hips. He looked to her as she bit down on her tongue at the corner of her mouth and began milking him with both her hands. Up and down with a soft twist that was slow and deliberate.*

*Up to the hot, swollen tip and down to the thick, rock-hard base. Again and again.*

*"Alessandra," he moaned, wishing his hands were free to touch her.*

*"Alek," she said in return.*

*Up. Down. Again and again.*

*"Don't make me come," he begged, biting on the side of his tongue.*

*Up. Down. Again and again.*

*"Yet?" she asked, pausing her actions.*

*He agreed. "Yet."*

*She rose to her feet, her hair swinging forward as she looked down at him. "Am I everything you thought I would be?" she asked, twisting her body this way and that seductively.*

*Alek was transfixed by the sight of her. The moonlight framed her body, and the sight of her nipples and the plump mound pressed against the sheer material was mesmerizing. He grunted as he tried to tear free of his restraints.*

*"Am I everything you want?" she asked, turning and bringing her hands up her thighs to caress her exposed derriere as she looked back over her shoulder. "Everything you need?"*

*Her teasing made him hungry for her.*

*"Everything you desire?" she asked, turning again to cup her breasts and tease her hard nipples through the barely-there material.*

*"Come and get it," she taunted, using the arch of her bare foot to stroke his stiff inches.*

*He roared, his muscles tense as he brought his arms and legs up off the bed, futilely straining against the cotton ties holding him captive to the bed...*

"Alessandra!"

Alek awakened, raising his head from the pillow to look down the length of his body at his hardness tenting the sheets. Still somewhere between fully awake and asleep, his face was bewildered as he looked left and right to find his arms open wide across his pillow, but free of any ties like his all-too-real vision.

Relaxing his body, he closed his eyes and released a heavy breath. His dream had been vivid. And in those moments as he waited for his erection to ease and his pulse to diminish, he wished like hell that he hadn't awakened.

# *Chapter 5*

*Simply amazing.*

"Pull over for a second, Roje," Alessandra said, sitting up in her seat of the back of the Jaguar.

"Yes, ma'am." He pulled the car to a stop on the curving road seemingly carved out of the mountain looming beside it.

As soon the vehicle stopped she climbed out and moved to stand at the metal railing lining the winding road. The smell of trees and earth was heavy as she looked in the distance at the view of the Lake House, seemingly nestled inside the towering trees and mountains of the Catskills with its reflection mirrored on the surrounding lake. Over the years since ADG acquired the once-small resort, the property had increased in size with more than three hundred guest rooms and suites. The additions maintained the original aesthetic of the stone castle with its pointed forest green rooftops referencing its surroundings.

It was picture-perfect.

Looking at it, for a moment, all her nerves about her presentation to the board that morning eased a bit.

"Are we having a moment, Alessandra? Please don't jump, sweetheart. There are way less messy ways to go."

*Poof.* The moment was gone with the same finality of a popped balloon.

She released a little moan of annoyance before looking over her shoulder at her aunt Leonora's head peeking out the rear window of one of the two Rolls-Royce Phantoms following behind her car. She wasn't surprised by the platinum flask clutched in her hand. Aunt Leonora enjoyed a good cocktail, and the alcohol made her tongue straight reckless.

Her father had been all about family, and his financial support of them had passed on to Alessandra upon his death. She loved them all, but they were quite a handful. She walked back to the car, careful not to trip on an errant rock or crack in the country road as she bent to look in the rear of the Phantom.

There was her aunt Brunela, her father's sister whom Alessandra recently put on a spending budget. She had made it clear that if she had been a man that the family business would have been hers to inherit and not her younger brother. And she seemed intent on spending as much as she could. The purchase of a five-million-dollar antique car had been a bit much, particularly when Brunela had never acquired a driver's license. *As if spending the family fortune would replace never being put in control of it.*

And Aunt Leonora, her father's younger sister who never married or had children. She had become Alessandra's mother figure in the years after her passing. Leonora's opinion and personality were much bigger than her petite stature, but she gave good advice and was a soft place for Alessandra to land when the world felt tough and unrelenting. *Even if her honesty sometimes stings.*

Alessandra eyed her cousin Marisa, lightly snoring in the corner with earphones plugged in, undoubtedly sleeping off another late night of partying and manhunting. She and Brunela's daughter were the same age but so completely different. Marisa had never been given the same responsibility and it was clear that her mother's overindulgence had not prepared her for adulthood. *She has the freedom to mess up. Lucky girl.*

Her father's first cousin, Victor, and his sixth wife, Elisabetta, and their toddler twins were in the last car. Although he was quite experienced at getting married, he was the worst possible candidate for a husband. Elisabetta was thirty years his junior and loved being his wife, so much so that she couldn't seem to be bothered to discipline their twin toddlers who were as bad as the day was long. They were quite a little family and Alessandra wished them well. Although Victor was employed by ADG and received a hefty salary, he had yet to make an appearance in his office in the last twenty years. *God help him the day Elisabetta realizes he spends his days test-driving wife number seven.*

"I was taking a little time to enjoy the view," she finally said.

"Well, who the hell are you, Barbara Walters?" Leonora asked, easing her flask back inside her Louis Vuitton tote.

Alessandra just laughed as she turned back to head to her car. "Roje, let's get these people to their rooms," she said, her tone amused.

He chuckled. "Right away."

She picked up her iPad from the seat beside her, settling back as she continued to prep for her presentation at the board meeting.

"You're ready, you know."

Alessandra looked up to find Roje's dark eyes on her in the rearview mirror. "I wish I was sure about that."

"Your father was sure," Roje said. "Trust and believe in that."

Her emotions swelled inside her like a crescendo and she shifted her eyes away. "Yes, he did, didn't he?" she asked with the hint of a smile.

Roje said nothing else. He didn't need to. His words were few but meaningful. He had been her father's driver for many years and he knew both Frances Dalmount and his daughter very well. There was a lot to learn from the front seat of a chauffeured car by a man willing to listen.

Alessandra closed the cover of her iPad and slid it into the side pocket of her alligator Saint Laurent Sac de Jour bag. It was her first visit to the luxury castle resort, and during the two hour drive the gradual transformation from urban landscapes to acres of forest had been surreal. It was a decided change from the tall skyscrapers and frenetic pace of Manhattan.

She was looking forward to the weekend of activities and relaxation. The last five years had moved with a speed that left her bone-tired and weary at night, with her shoes kicked off and her feet up on the antique French provincial table. Some celebrating and taking some time to slow down and enjoy life wouldn't be a bad thing at all.

*But first, let's get this business out of the way...*

As Roje turned the Jaguar up the stone driveway, it was hard not to be impressed by the grandeur, scope and size of the resort. It was a gem in the ADG portfolio, and Alessandra could admit she was pleased with Alek's choice to hold their festivities there.

She slid on her shades and climbed from the car with Roje's assistance. She glanced at her watch and looked up. Her eyes widened a bit at the sight of Alek and his equally handsome brother helping his mother and sister from the rear of a black Maybach 62. She'd never seen him in casual clothing, and the dark blue button-up shirt he wore with distressed denims and brown burnished leather drivers looked really good against his chocolate complexion. His aviator shades shielded his expression from her when he looked up and saw her, but he stared for a long enough moment to make her gasp softly.

She looked away first.

Alessandra was surprised to discover that Roje still stood behind her. It wasn't like him to linger. She followed his line of vision to find his eyes resting on LuLu Ansah, Alek's mother, who looked stunning in a deep purple wrap shirt paired with white linen pants. A woman it would be hard to tell was in her midfifties, she always had a regal air about her that Alessandra found fascinating, and her head wrap in colors of purple and gold seemed like a crown on her head.

"Everything okay, Roje?" Alessandra asked, biting the inside of her cheek to keep from smiling.

He cleared his throat and stroked his mouth and white goatee with a hand before turning his attention to the Jaguar and finally getting in and closing the door.

"Alessandra, it's really nice to see you again."

She faced Alek and his family walking up to her. Out of respect for his mother, she stepped forward to meet them halfway. "Thank you, Ms. Ansah. It's good to see to you," she said warmly, pressing a kiss to both of the woman's cheeks and ignoring Alek standing beside his mother and staring at her.

Alessandra remembered his frustration with her just the day before and hoped it didn't linger. A weekend of Alek scowling at her at every turn would just ruin the entire celebration. *As would the board voting to implement his acquisition.*

She smiled and nodded at both Samira and Naim, both standing there looking like models in a Gucci magazine ad. "Alek," she said, acknowledging him.

He leaned forward to press his lips to her cheeks. "How are you, Alessandra?" he asked.

She covered her surprise as his well-groomed beard tickled her face a bit. "I'm good, and you?" she asked, her tone polite.

LuLu chuckled. "You two are a mess, but your politeness is very civilized," she said, her accent heavy.

Alek leaned back from her. "I'll make sure the rooms are ready," he said, looking back at his brother. "Come on, Naim."

Samira stepped forward, looking pretty in a peach

strapless sundress. "I am very impressed by you, Ms. Dalmount," she said.

"Call me Alessandra," she offered. "We're not that far apart in age."

She shrugged one mahogany-brown shoulder. "But you are in profession, so it doesn't seem that way," Samira said, easing her thick straight hair over the other shoulder.

Alessandra was confused by that statement and it reflected on her face.

Samira smiled, showing a deep dimple in her left cheek. "My brother won't allow me to work for the company as a relative," she said, her annoyance displayed in her tone if not in her eyes.

"That sounds about right," Alessandra said lightly, not wanting to fuel a family disagreement even as her own annoyance at Alek's chauvinistic beliefs surfaced.

"Perhaps you can give me the chance he won't," she said, her eyes serious as she reached out to hand Alessandra a thick cream envelope.

She took it from her, looking down at the woman's name embossed in gold.

"My résumé," Samira said.

Alessandra looked back up at her. She was no more than twenty-one or twenty-two, but she was everything Alessandra pretended to be, particularly fearless. At Samira's continued silence, Alessandra looked to her mother to gauge her take on her daughter's open defiance of Alek.

Ms. Ansah stood there with them, but her attention was elsewhere.

Alessandra glanced over her shoulder.

Roje stood there, a respectful distance back from them, and LuLu's eyes were on him.

She turned back to Samira, leaving them to whatever business they were creating. "I'm not sure what I can do, but I will look this over, maybe make some recommendation to colleagues in the industry," she said.

Samira shook her head. "I want to work for the firm my grandfather created from nothing and my father helped shape into a billion-dollar corporation," she said. "I want in at ADG."

The glass ceiling was still in full effect in corporate America, particularly for women of color. Even with the past advancements of CEOs like Rosalind Brewer at Starbucks, Ursula Burns at Xerox, Indra Nooyi at PepsiCo, Debra Lee at BET, and now herself at ADG, Alessandra realized she had joined an unspoken club of unicorns who were able to excel in spite of adversity.

Her own time at ADG had not been easy, but she was well aware in the current corporate climate that she still had not put in the work of her peers. Nepotism could not be denied as having some role in her success, nor could her business acumen.

Not in Alek's or Naim's careers, either, though.

Didn't Samira deserve the same?

Alessandra stiffened her back and squared her shoulders as she extended her hand to the younger woman. "Let me see what I can do," she said.

"That's all I ask," Samira said.

"Okay, ladies, I have to prepare for a board meeting," she said, giving Samira's hand a squeeze.

LuLu was now refocused on them, but her eyes were distant, as if she wished to be somewhere else.

Alessandra glanced back to find Roje supervising the removal of her luggage from the Jaguar. Her family's drivers had already done so and were gone, with her family now entering the resort. Alessandra turned to do the same, tucking Samira's envelope inside her tote.

"Yes, let's go inside," Samira said, following Alessandra.

LuLu followed behind them. "I didn't eat breakfast and I could eat something," she said, sounding distracted.

"The food is supposed to be delicious," she said, turning to glance back just as Ms. Ansah and Roje lightly touched hands as she passed by him.

"I love my brother, Alessandra," Samira said, as they crossed the lobby. "But good luck."

"Thank you," Alessandra returned earnestly, turning away from the small but telling moment.

Alek was in his element as he ran across the red clay tennis courts to swing his racket with force and accuracy to lob the ball. The onlookers applauded as the ball shot over his opponent and landed inside the line for the win. He raised his racket high above his head and balled his free hand into a fist to pump the air vigorously as he raced up the court.

Garrison Wyndham let out a shout of frustration as he spun his racket, coming up to the net. "Good win, Alek," he said, sweat plastering his blond hair to his head. "That wasn't retaliation for the board meeting, was it?"

Alek smiled as they shook hands. "Maybe a little," he joked, accepting the monogrammed towel from a middle-school-aged ball boy. "A win is a win, and I needed one after that loss a couple of days ago."

Garrison wiped his face and neck, leveling blue eyes on Alek. "It wasn't a loss, Alek. You both had strong presentations and the votes were evenly split, leaving it at a standoff."

Alek just shrugged as he wrapped the towel around his neck and tucked the ends inside the V-neck of his T-shirt. "It may be time to push the board to vote on her removal."

"*Or* you both can do what we suggested, in the tradition of the compromise for which your fathers were known, and decide together whose plan goes forward," Garrison offered.

"I'm going to shower and then get some lunch," Alek said, now done with the conversation. "See you at the ball?"

Garrison nodded, acknowledging the abrupt change in conversation. "My wife and I are taking the kids kayaking. They're disappointed the ball is adult only."

"Enjoy," he said, forcing warmth into his voice.

He wasn't angry about the board's decision and didn't want to appear that way.

"We will," Garrison said before walking away.

Alek turned and followed suit. He smiled when Millicent came through the plexiglass gate of the glass fence surrounding one of the eight tennis courts on the property. Onlookers sat at wrought iron tables enjoying the game or just having lunch in the floral settings.

He shoved his racket inside the bag and zipped it as he smiled at her in welcome. He'd known her since her modeling days in Paris and they'd dated often. When he learned she had moved to New York he decided to reconnect with the beauty and invite her as his date for just the ball. He was pleased she agreed because he didn't want the constraint of having a date there for the entire four-day weekend.

"Congratulations, Alek," she called over to him, looking like pure sunshine in the yellow sundress she wore with her reddish-brown hair blowing in the wind behind her.

His smile faded. Over Millicent's shoulder he spotted Alessandra walking onto the court followed by her date. His jaw clenched and the heat of jealousy burned his gut when she looked up at the man and laughed with such abandon that she seemed to radiate. The very presence of the man had irked his spirit since he first learned of his arrival the night before.

He had been distracted with the thought of them sharing her double-level suite until he checked with the front desk to ensure he had his own room. Ownership had its privileges.

He took in the sight of her in a white halter tennis tank that showed just a sliver of skin at her waist and a matching skirt with a hem that cut right across the top of her shapely thighs. That tiny sliver and the length of her legs was enough for him to overlook Millicent crossing the court to reach him until she was standing directly in front of him.

He jumped in surprise as she pressed a kiss to his cheek above his beard. "When did you get in?" he asked.

"This morning," she said.

"You like your room?" he asked.

"And *all* of the amenities," she said with a coy smile. "I had a stone massage and a facial that was absolutely beyond anything I've ever had. Kudos to the owner."

"You mean co-owner."

Alek's and Alessandra's eyes locked over Millicent's shoulder before she turned around. "I didn't mean anything—"

Alessandra grabbed her hand and smiled comfortingly. "I was just trying to pick at Alek," she reassured her.

"That sounds about right," Alek said, extending his hand past Alessandra to her date. "Alek Ansah."

"Hill Graham," he answered.

Alek gave his hand an extra firm grip and then felt petty when the man visibly winced.

Alessandra's eyes went from the men's hands and up to Alek's eyes with a slight arch to one of her eyebrows.

"We'll see you later," he said, lightly pressing his hand to Millicent's lower back to guide her past them.

"You really looked good out there, Alek," Millicent told him.

He barely heard her. His thoughts were somewhere else. Or rather on someone else.

As he held the gate open for her to step through, he glanced back. His breath caught to find Alessandra looking past Hill with her eyes resting on him.

They held that stare. Time seemed to tick by slowly.

*"Am I everything you want?"*

*"Everything you need?"*

*"Everything you desire?"*

"Let's go kayaking," Millicent said from somewhere outside the bubble.

"Alek. Alek? Alek!"

Millicent shook his arm roughly, jarring him. He looked down at her in question. "Huh?"

"Is everything okay?" she asked, lightly touching his chest.

"Yes," he lied, gently steering her from the tennis court as he forced himself not to look back again.

As she stood in a dress most women would crave wearing, Alessandra had never felt so unsure in her life. She pressed a trembling hand to her stomach as she eased the black curtain open just enough to peek out at the transformed east dining room of the Lake House. She smiled at the ADG employees and their spouses, dates and adult family members enjoying the live band and the elegant decor of the candlelight, warm white lighting and colorful floral arrangements on each table contrasting with the dark wood of the ceiling and the stone pillars.

The venue's event planners had done a wonderful job and she was pleased.

*And nervous.*

A frown marred her brow when she spotted her cousin Marisa in the middle of the dance floor with her hands high above her head as she danced to "Wild Thoughts" by DJ Khaled and Rihanna, drawing attention as the skirt of her short sequined dress rose high on her legs. She winced as the wife of the telecommunications director jerked his arm when he started to dance up to Marisa as she bent over and wiggled her bottom.

*I know she didn't. No to the hell no.*

She turned to look over her shoulder and spotted the resort's lead event planner in the wings of the stage reviewing something on her clipboard. "Cindy," Alessandra called out in a loud whisper.

The woman looked up and immediately walked over to where Alessandra stood behind the closed curtains. "We're just waiting on Mr. Ansah and we'll be ready to make the announcement and free you from back here," she said, her tone congenial.

"No, I'm fine, I just need you, or one of your staff, to go to the woman putting on the show in the middle of the floor and tell her *I* said for her plant her ass in a seat or she can go *home*," Alessandra stressed, pulling back the curtain to point out Marisa. "And let her know I am *so* serious about this."

Cindy's expression became pained after she peeked past the silk curtain. That spoke volumes that Alessandra was not overreacting. "Right away," she said, swiftly walking back into the wings and down the stairs leading to the dining room.

Alessandra watched on as Cindy reached her cousin and discreetly guided her from the dance floor as she spoke into her ear. Marisa did not look pleased, but she immediately reclaimed her seat next to her mother at their round table. Alessandra had no doubt that she would do as she bid. Being the one to dole out the family allowances had its privileges.

Waiters filed in carrying crystal flutes of Armand de Brignac champagne, ensuring every person was handed a glass. Alessandra wasn't surprised when Marisa insisted on two. Her life was always about excess. Everything was too much: too much drinking, too much partying and too many men.

"If you're looking for me, I'm right here, Alessandra."

Her body froze as her pulse raced, and she closed her eyes as she quickly sought control. Turning, she was surprised to find Alek standing so close behind her. He wore all black with a tuxedo obviously tailored for just his frame. His eyes seemed more intense. The cut of his jaw with his trimmed beard more masculine. His supple lips more enticing. Just handsome. Devastatingly so.

She took a step back. The curtain swayed.

He reached out to press his hands to her bare upper arms to steady her. "Damn, Alessandra," he said as his eyes moved up and down the length of her body in pure appreciation.

The sound of the Latin-flavored music was haunting. The lyrics spoke to temptation.

She was breathless. All her fears and nerves about her dress faded into the heat of his clear approval of her choice. The custom sheer figure-hugging backless gown with a plunging neckline was showered with crystal embellishments that sparkled beneath the overhead lights. Her glam squad had her hair piled atop her head, exposing her neck, and her makeup was a dark and dramatic smoky eye with a nude lip.

But it wasn't until that moment, as Alek looked down at her with hunger in his eyes, that she felt beautiful. Her nipples hardened against the dress as she fought so hard to continue fighting the tension that swelled between them, sometimes under the pretense of anger. But it was pure attraction. Heat. Desire. Want.

It pulsed with a life all its own whenever they were near each other.

In that moment, Alessandra couldn't think of one reason to fight it any longer.

"Alek," she breathed, reaching up to grip the lapels of his tuxedo in her greedy little hands as she stepped closer to him.

His grasp on her arms tightened as he lowered his head to hers.

*Yes. Let me see if your mouth feels as soft as it looks, Alek.*

Rapid footsteps echoed and they jumped apart just before Cindy came across the stage to reach them.

The moment was gone.

Their regret was palpable.

"Okay, if you both can move center stage," Cindy said as a waiter approached with a tray with two flutes of champagne. "As soon as this last song stops playing, Mr. Brent will come up onstage, introduce you both, and the curtains will open."

Alek barely heard the woman as he accepted the flute and moved to the spot she indicated. He glanced back at Alessandra as she did the same and was as mesmerized by the sight of her in that dress as he was when she first turned around to face him. He took a sip of the champagne to steady himself.

"Okay, good luck," Cindy said, before disappearing and leaving them alone again.

Alessandra came to stand beside him, glancing up at him.

Their eyes locked.

There it was again. That shift in the space-time continuum. Everything seemed to go still around them as they were in tune with each other.

Alek turned to face her. His heart pounded with such force. Little Alessandra the shy girl had grown into a woman who had the power to weaken his knees with a touch. His eyes searched hers, and the desire he felt for her was mirrored. "Alessandra," he said, low in his throat, as he dropped his head to hers again.

She brought her free hand up to stroke his beard as she raised up on her toes to meet his mouth with her own.

Alek's entire body felt alive with awareness as they kissed. Her mouth was just as sweet and soft as he imagined. His face tingled where she stroked his cheek. With a moan in the back of his throat, he slowly deepened the kiss and brought his free hand up to her back to press her body forward against his.

He felt her tremble from his touch. It made him heady. He sucked the tip of her tongue, and her moan of pleasure pushed him over the edge. He lowered his hand to grip one fleshy cheek of her buttocks.

He had never felt so alive.

"Good evening, ADG family!" Aldrich Brent roared into the microphone.

Alek placed soft kisses around her gaping mouth, leaning down to kiss and tease her neck, caring nothing about the acrid taste of her sultry perfume.

"Oh, Alek," she sighed, tilting her head back in abandon. "Yes. Yes. *Yes*."

"I know Frances and Kwame are here in spirit celebrating this momentous occasion. It was clearly their wish for their children to run this business together just as they did starting thirty years ago this week," Aldrich continued, his voice echoing around them.

Alek offered her his tongue.

She looked up at him as she sucked it.

Never had he wanted to be inside a woman so badly.

"Without further delay it is time to introduce the leaders of the Ansah Dalmount Group as they lead our corporation into an even brighter and more successful future with the same vision, drive and ambition passed on to them by their respective fathers," Aldrich said. "Rise and let us welcome the owners and chief executive officers of the Ansah Dalmount Group… Alessandra Dalmount and Alek Ansah!"

Someone cleared their throat. And then cleared it again. And again.

Alessandra and Alek were lost in each other.

"The curtain!"

They broke apart at the shriek, finding Cindy standing in the wings waving at them frantically as the curtain quickly opened from the left of the stage.

Alek and Alessandra shared a look as the energy they created dissipated like a mist.

"Wipe your mouth," she told him as she straightened her dress.

He did so with his thumb, feeling the sticky gloss on his lips.

The curtain swept past them and they both stepped forward with a smile, their champagne-filled flutes raised high in the air as the thunderous applause surrounded them.

From her spot at the front of the applauding crowd, LuLu Ansah squinted her eyes as she spotted the hint of sheer pink gloss on the corner of her son's mouth and cheek as he finished giving a speech promising a bright future for ADG. She shifted her attention to Alessandra standing a respectful distance from him and looking on with poise and respect.

But her hair was slightly disheveled and her mouth was free of any lipstick or gloss.

*Well, well...*

That amused her, and she couldn't help but smile as she rushed forward to wrap her arms around them both and pulled their heads in close as she hugged them. "Alessandra, your gloss is missing, sweet one, and somehow, it's on my son's mouth," she teased for their ears alone with a chuckle.

Alessandra stiffened. LuLu warmly rubbed her shoulder like only a mother could.

Alek immediately turned and removed his black linen handkerchief to wipe his mouth. LuLu chuckled again.

She stepped back from them and allowed their dates, family, colleagues and employees swell forward to congratulate them. Alek and Alessandra? She wasn't surprised. She'd seen it coming a mile away. Their level of animosity for each other was unnatural, and the root cause for that level of annoyance was always passion denied.

She knew quite a bit about that.

LuLu stopped a waiter for a new flute of champagne from his tray. "Thank you so much," she said with a bow of her head, before she continued out of the dining room and onto the wood terrace surrounding the entire building. She inhaled deeply of the fresh air before taking a deep sip of her drink, leaving her bright red lipstick on the rim as she did.

"You have never looked more beautiful, LuLu."

*Roje.*

Surprise and pleasure filled her.

She turned. "Same to you," she said, taking in the

navy suit he wore with a matching open button-up beneath it.

"LuLu—"

She smiled sadly and shook her head. "Roje, I can't," she said softly. "That one night helped me heal. Even a year after Kwame's death I was so lost. What we shared helped me forget for a little while, but I can't. And you know that. So, please, Roje. *Please*."

His eyes were filled with his regret, but he nodded.

She walked past him, but he stepped in her path. "That night I left a piece of my heart with you that I will never get back, LuLu," he said. "I just want you to know that."

For a moment, they went back in time to that long passionate night they shared in his bed.

LuLu pressed a kiss to the side of his mouth. "So did I, Roje," she admitted in a whisper, before moving past him and walking away with regrets.

# Chapter 6

Alessandra could not sleep.

Memories of the passion she shared with Alek haunted her. Passion that had been stoked for weeks. Passion that may very well be hard to douse. It felt like dropping a lit match to a trail of gasoline and then trying to avoid the explosion that was to follow.

*What happens now?*

For the rest of the night they watched each other from across the room, unable to deny the intense attraction.

*What now?*

She flung back the sheets and rose from the king-size bed to cross the spacious suite and step out the wood-trimmed doors lining the room to her balcony. A warm summer breeze blew against the black lace nightgown she wore. She looked out at the moon reflected against the mountain lake. Not even the picturesque view could calm her raging emotions. At first there was pleasure that Alek couldn't seem to resist her any more than she was able to deny her attraction to him. And then there was remorse for so desperately wanting a man who didn't respect her presence in the business world simply because she was a woman.

As she remembered their fiery kiss, she touched her lips with a trembling hand. "What's wrong with me?" she said out loud, truly puzzled.

"The same thing that's wrong with me."

Alessandra was startled. She looked over to find Alek on the balcony directly to her left. She hadn't known his suite was next to hers, but it made sense they would be given the best accommodations at the resort. Her eyes took in the sight of him in nothing but navy silk pajama bottoms that hung low on his narrow hips and clung to the lengthy curve of him as he came to the end of his balcony nearly connecting with hers.

His eyes, those dark, intense eyes, were locked on her as he began to climb over the very short divide between their balconies.

"Alek," she said, her heart pounding and pulse racing as she backed away as if the distance would ease her desire for him.

He shook his head as if to say "Hell, no," as he strode over to pull her into his arms and without a bit of hesitation captured her mouth with his own.

She pressed her hands against the smooth brown skin of his chest and shoulder, but her resistance was weak and soon she kissed him back as she eased her hands up to press to the back of his head. His body, the strength and the heat, felt so good against her softness. His chest to her breasts. The length of his hardness against her belly.

He used his strength to pick her up into his arms.

Alessandra stroked his arms, loving the feel of his muscles flexing. Her core warmed more and she moaned as the pulsing bud snuggled inside her lips ached for release.

He walked them into the coolness of her suite and pressed their bodies to one of the large club chairs before the balcony doors, with no patience to reach the bed as they gave in to their craving for each other. Alek shifted her body to one side to caress and stroke her thighs as he pressed his face to her neck, feeling her racing pulse against his lips.

Alessandra was no innocent—she had experienced passion before—but nothing prepared her for the chemistry she created with Alek. Nothing. She arched her back up off the chair, gasping for breath and seeking relief from her body feeling so electrified. "Alek," she sighed, spreading her legs wide and lifting one over his hip when he hitched the hem of her delicate nightgown up to her thighs.

He looked down into her face framed by the moonlight as he palmed her core, his fingertips resting in the soft divide of her buttocks, as he massaged her deeply, pressing the fleshy part of his palm against her moist clit. "Feels good?" he asked her, his voice thick with his yearning.

"Yes," she admitted in a heated rush, pressing one foot against the arm of the chair to rotate her hips against his hand.

She lifted her head from the back of the chair to lick hotly at his mouth before she bit his bottom lip.

He grunted in pleasure.

Alessandra smiled a little as she ran her tongue inside the softness of his mouth before he tangled his own with hers. She reached for his hardness, caressing him from midway to the smooth tip as he lowered his head to suck deeply at her hard nipple through the Venetian lace. Down she stroked and then up, using the side of her thumb to softly stroke the tip.

He swore, freeing himself from her grasp just long enough to snatch off his pajama bottoms and then stand before her.

Alessandra grabbed him with both hands as she looked up at him. "It's so big," she whispered up to him in awe, before she leaned in to lick the tip.

His legs stiffened and he cried out as he flung his head back.

*Knock-knock.*

She froze, looking back over her shoulder at the door to her suite.

"It's Hill. Are you awake, Alessandra?" her date called through the closed door before knocking again.

"Damn," Alek swore in frustration, his long and curving length bobbing a bit as she released it. "*This* fool."

Alessandra shook her head as if to clear it as she rose to press past Alek's nude frame. "Just go, Alek," she pleaded in a whisper, her eyes dropping to take in the sight of his rock-hard body with his erection hanging from his body with a curve that looked dangerous.

*Did I really lick it?*

She thought of Alek's cry of pleasure.

*Yes, I did, and I liked it.*

"Am I interrupting something?" he asked, his voice hard and accusing.

"No," she emphasized. "I don't even know what he wants."

"I'm not going anywhere," he insisted, massaging the length of his erection with one hand as he reached for her with the other. "Ignore him."

"No," she insisted, moving quickly even as her body reacted to him. "You just have to realize how inappropriate this all looks. Remember, Millicent?"

His face said that he hadn't. "She's in her own room and I have no intention of seeing her until morning."

"Alek! A tryst with me tonight and breakfast with your date in the morning? What the hell kind of woman do you think I am?" Alessandra snapped angrily, bending down to scoop up his discarded pajama bottoms before pushing against his chest until he backed out onto the balcony. She flung them into his face. "Just go away, Alek. Good night."

She slammed the balcony door and locked it.

Relief flooded her when he casually draped the pajamas over one broad shoulder and strolled away to climb back over to his own balcony.

Alek rushed across his spacious suite, stubbing his toe against an antique coffee table. He hollered as he reached the door, pausing just long enough to pull on his pajamas before he eased the door open and looked down the long hall.

Hill, dressed in his pants and shirt, was still at Alessandra's door knocking with a bottle of brown liquor and two snifters in his free hand. *A nightcap? Yeah, right.*

Alek's frown changed into a big and broad smile; he leaned against the door frame and crossed his arms over his chest. "Everything okay?" he called.

Hill turned and smiled. "Yes, everything is fine," he said, turning back to the door.

Alek remained.

Hill glanced back at him. "Everything okay with you, Alek?" he asked, his annoyance with him clear.

He shrugged. "Your knocking kinda woke me," he said with a little wince. "I'm pretty sure if I hear it way down here she has to hear from right there. Right, kid?"

Hill forced a smile, giving Alessandra's door one last glance before he walked away.

Alek was gleeful. When the other man reached him he quickly reached out to grab one of the snifters. "Nightcap? I surely could use one," he hinted, holding the glass out.

Hill released a heavy breath as he opened the small round decanter to fill Alek's snifter.

"Thanks. Good night, Hill," Alek said with way too much glee.

Hill gave him a stiff nod before continuing down the hall to the elevator, eventually climbing on it and disappearing behind the closed doors.

Alek drank all the brandy in one gulp and entered his suite with a chuckle.

"Everything okay, Alessandra?"

She looked at Roje's concerned expression in the rearview mirror of the Jaguar MK VII sedan. She smiled at him reassuringly. "It is now that I'm home," she said, turning to look out the window at the large bronze sign welcoming them to Passion Grove, New Jersey.

The population of the town, home of many wealthy young millennials, was under two thousand with fewer than three hundred homes, each on an average of five or more acres. Its name was derived from the township being centered on a heart-shaped lake that the residents lounged around in the summer and skated on in the winter.

There were no apartment buildings or office buildings. Not even public transportation through the town. The township had tight restrictions on commercial activity to maintain the small-town feel. Each of the tree-lined, brick-paved streets was named after a flower. Care was given to its beautification, with large pots on each street corner filled with plants or colorful perennial florae.

Alessandra had grown up there and couldn't imagine moving. Now that the majority of her life was sucked into the fast pace of Manhattan, Passion Grove had truly become her respite.

As Roje drove her through the downtown area, she smiled at its comparison to Manhattan and other metropolitan cities. Most of the businesses were in small converted homes that were relics from its incorporation in the early 1900s. The police station, a gourmet grocery store that delivered, a few high-end boutiques, a dog groomer, and a concierge service that supplied luxuries not available in town.

The streets lacked the constant movement of people, and traffic was minimal at best. No highways or traffic lights. The stop sign sufficed.

A few neighbors enjoying coffee and pastries on

the sidewalk outside the bakery waved at her as they passed. In the city people waved, too, but usually their hand displayed only one finger at the time.

Passion Grove was home, and when she awakened that morning with memories of her lack of inhibitions with Alek, she had wanted nothing more than to be back in a place where she felt the most like herself. The most comfortable. The most familiar.

When she asked Alek to leave it had nothing to do with Hill's ridiculous appearance at her door. She used that intrusion to gain some clarity and give herself the distance needed from Alek…and his touch, his kisses and his hardness.

Hill's late-night intentions at her door were clear but she spared him a tongue-lashing and just ignored his knocks because she was thankful for his intrusion. He had unknowingly saved her from losing every last bit of her sense and control by having sex with her nemesis. She poured herself a stiff shot of some brown liquor from her bar in the suite and went back to bed, trying hard not to wish Alek was there with her. And in her. Deeply.

Alessandra sighed.

She had run from Alek yet again.

Early in the morning before the sun fully rose in the sky and everything was still, she had called Roje in his room downstairs and rushed into clothes. No time was wasted to summon the resort's maid to assist her, and she shoved the rest of her costly designer frocks inside her suitcase. She flew, knowing she was missing the early-afternoon brunch signaling the end of the weekend-long celebration. In her haste, she left Hill and her family behind.

*Everyone's grown with vehicles. No one is stranded.*

From behind her rimless shades Alessandra looked out the left passenger-side tinted window at the sun glistening on the lake. Even with the distance from the street, she could see a small fishing boat and knew it was Lance Millner, a local reclusive author, who fished every morning.

Roje made the left turn down Dalmount Lane, the private mile-long paved street leading to their sprawling twenty-five-acre estate. Her father commissioned a one-of-a-kind hybrid rose in honor of her mother that he named the Dalmount, which made it eligible to be the name of the private street. Soon she spotted the twelve-foot-tall wrought iron gate with the letter *D* in bronzed scroll in the center. Roje pulled up to the security panel and lowered his window to enter his pass code.

Moments later the gates rolled open and he eased forward with a brief wave to the security guard on duty who monitored the gate by video surveillance from the mansion. It was another half mile down a tree-lined paved road before the three-story, 24,000-square-foot stone French Tudor came into view. To the left he passed the six-car attached garage with the security office above it before following the curved driveway in front of the mansion. Roje made the left to steer the Jaguar under the carport where deliveries were made, passing the side entrance leading directly into the gourmet kitchen and continuing down the long path to the 1,500-square-foot guest cottage.

Alessandra smiled.

The estate had many amenities, including an

Olympic-size infinity swimming pool centered to the rear of the mansion with a four-thousand-square-foot pool house behind it. There were also outdoor tennis courts, a basketball court, an indoor and outdoor home theater, an outdoor kitchen and a horse stable. The rear of her family's estate overlooked the public lake, and there was a landing with two bowrider boats for fishing or water sports.

Even with all of that it was the little guest cottage with three bedrooms and two and a half baths that was her happy place. She rushed from the back of the car before Roje could leave the driver's seat and assist her. She heard him chuckle as she zoomed past him to open the door and raced inside, barely noting the way the bright light of the summer sun bounced off the neutral decor with pops of bright color and wood accents.

She entered her bedroom suite, kicking off her leopard-print heels as she reached behind her to unzip her strapless crimson Valentino jumpsuit—it was the first of Shiva's garment bags she grabbed in the darkness that morning to put on. Next went the bra.

"Your luggage, Ms. Dalmount," Roje called from the front doorway.

She began unclipping the tracks from her hair. "Enjoy the rest of your day off, Roje," she called back, before digging her fingers into her own hair and massaging her scalp.

Alessandra heard the front door close securely.

"Yesssss," she sighed, naked and feeling free as she entered her en suite to remove her thong. Although she wore no makeup, she scrubbed her face with her favorite skin-care regimen.

When she finally emerged from her guesthouse via

the side entrance, she had on cutoff shorts and a tank top, her shoulder-length hair was in an unruly ponytail, and she wore her favorite tortoiseshell round spectacles that always slipped down to the tip of her nose. Barefoot, she made her way to her small fenced-in garden. Her smile was full and bright as she felt the warm earth between her toes before she knelt to begin tending to her vegetables.

Soon perspiration coated her body and she used the back of her forearm to wipe the sweat from her brow as she tilted her head back to accept the rays of the sun.

Peace reigned.

Her equilibrium was restored.

This was her happy place to decompress from the stressors of her family life and her career, and to enjoy some semblance of the life she wished she'd been able to claim as her own. Here she relished her privacy and was able to put away the facade she used to flourish in business. Here she was just Alex. Painting, reading and gardening were her joys.

"I needed this," Alessandra said, sitting back on her haunches to look across the small plot where she planted cucumbers.

They hung from the vine, long and thick, some curving a bit with the bundles of leaves surrounding them just like the soft hairs of a man's groin.

*Just like Alek*, she thought.

She shook her head to clear it of the all-too-vivid memory of the sight of his nudity.

She failed.

*It's so big.*

Alessandra felt her face flush at the memory of her

words just before she leaned in to lick the tip of him. Her core warmed at how he had cried out as he flung his head back.

"Damn it," she swore, rising to her feet in frustration that she couldn't free herself of wanting Alek Ansah.

She snatched off her gloves, making her way back up the path to her house as she pulled her iPhone from her back pocket to check the time. Hours had passed. It was late afternoon. She looked up the drive to the main house. *Are they back?*

Alessandra dropped her gloves onto the cedar bench running along the side of the house. Her family was loud and boisterous. It was normally the last thing she was looking for on her weekends off, but maybe sitting back and watching the top-rated Bravo reality show that they could be would keep thoughts of Alek off her mind.

She walked over to the all-black golf cart parked in front of her two-car garage and drove it up the path to the main house. She jerked her foot down on the brake at the sight of her cousin Victor's twin boys standing on the balcony of their parent's suite urinating. Elisabetta was flipping through a glossy magazine and smoking an e-cigarette as she relaxed on a padded lounge chair and basically ignored her toddlers.

"Hello, Alessandra," the boys yelled when they spotted her, both tossing water balloons as they stuck out their tongues.

Elisabetta looked up and waved her hand before returning her attention to her magazine.

She opened her mouth to reprimand the children

and their mother, but then shut it. "You know what," she mumbled. "Not today. Not one bit of it. Hell no."

She continued up the drive but stopped again at the sight of Marisa, naked as she pleased, jumping into the pool. Her left eye started twitching and her hands gripped the steering wheel, wishing it were her cousin's neck.

This time she threw the golf cart in Reverse and headed back to the guesthouse. "I can't. I shan't. I won't."

*I can tomorrow, though, because it's time for a family meeting.*

She wouldn't tolerate her kindness being taken for weakness. There were no provisions in the will ordering her to financially take care of her extended family, and definitely nothing saying to let them have the mansion so that she could find peace and enjoy her solitude. She did it because her father had done so, but she had to make it clear that it was her goodwill that kept them all wealthy. Nothing else.

Back in her house, she turned her phones on silent, fixed a turkey sandwich with cranberry relish on a toasted brioche bun, and poured herself a large glass of Côte de Beaune Montrachet chardonnay before settling down on her sofa with a book from her crowded shelves flanking the stone fireplace. She was determined not to think of Alek—not even her disappointment over the board requesting they confer as the joint heads of the company and decide on who should concede. Neither Alek nor Alessandra would budge, so the vote was delayed, with an urging for them to compromise with each other.

*That battle would wait until tomorrow, too.*

She took a bite of her sandwich and a deep gulp of her wine.

*Knock-knock-knock-knock.*

Alessandra cut her eyes at the door and frowned. She closed her book and sat it on her sofa before she rose to cross the room. She opened the door. "Alek?" she said in confusion, before adamantly shaking her head and stepping back to close the door.

Alek quickly moved past his shock at the fresh-faced sight of Alessandra to step forward and block her from closing the door. "Alessandra, we need to talk," he insisted, surprised at the weight she placed against the door to keep him from opening any wider.

"How did you get past security?" she asked, not relenting in the pressure she put against the door.

"Your aunt Leonora gave them permission to let me past the gate," he said.

"Six figures a year for security just wasted," she mumbled in disgust.

"I'm not a threat, Alessandra," he insisted.

"Alek, just go. The way my life is set up right now I cannot deal with you today. Seriously, Alek," she stressed.

He closed his eyes, wondering if he should use his strength to overpower her and push the door open. He decided against it. "Alessandra, I'd rather we talk today than do it tomorrow at the office or even pretend last night never happened," he said, tempering his voice.

After a few moments of silence, the door opened and he stepped inside. He eyed her from ponytail to bare feet, pausing at the sight of the back-and-forth motion of her buttocks in her cutoff shorts as she crossed the room to pick up her glass of wine. This pared-down version was more like the little Alex he remembered, but still his appreciation of her was not diminished. Not one bit. He liked that she was capable of going from Instagram-model-level beauty to a regular girl just chilling at home with a fresh face.

She took a sip, looking at him over the rim.

His heart tugged. She was adorable. He looked around her living room, searching for a distraction from the butterflies in his stomach.

"One comment on my appearance, today or any other day, and I will spare no cost to find out something just as embarrassing about you," Alessandra told him with a hard stare over the top of her glasses as she sat down, tucking one foot beneath her bottom.

"You have no reason to be, Alessandra," he said, coming around the living room to stand beside the sofa and look down at her.

*You're beautiful.*

His heart skipped a beat.

*What's wrong with me?*

"I think we both know last night was a mistake that we should blame on the alcohol and just move forward—"

"Our first drink was the champagne toast." He cut her off smoothly, denying her excuse.

Alessandra took another sip of wine and then placed her glass on the table. She looked nervous.

"And alcohol doesn't explain away the last few weeks, Alessandra," Alek reminded her, sliding his hands into the pockets of the denims he wore with a crisp white button-up shirt.

"What do you want, Alek?" she asked, rising to her

feet. "Because I can tell you that what I want from you has nothing to do with what happened last night. I can't earn my respect from you on my back. So I will not sleep with you, Alek. I will not. I won't. No."

He stepped close to her and instantly felt drawn into her. "Are you convincing yourself or me?"

Her gaze fell to his mouth but she jerked it back up to his eyes and took a step a back from him. "Both," she admitted softly. "I am your equal, your partner, and should be your ally but you have never wanted that even though I deserve it for so many reasons, Alek Ansah."

He bit his bottom lip and nodded his head, pushing away the desire to smooth away the tightness of her jaw. He moved over to the bottle of wine on the counter, seeking distance from her for his own clarity. "I was wrong, Alessandra," he confessed, his back to her as he noted her wine selection. "You have proven to be more adept at business than I thought."

"Say what now?" she asked in rush, the words blending together.

He looked over his shoulder and smiled at her shocked expression. He saw her stance soften, and she pressed her fingertips to the bridge of her nose.

"This has not been easy for me, Alek," she said, her eyes becoming bright with unshed tears. "I just need you to respect that. I won't lie. I was *so* afraid and... and I knew I had to work twice as hard as you, and I *did*. I couldn't fail. I *didn't* fail, Alek, even when everyone sat back and waited for me to fall flat on my face."

She closed her eyes and raised her face to the vaulted ceiling as she released a long and shaky breath and her shoulders drooped under the weight of her feelings.

A pain radiated across his chest as he forced himself not to go to her and pull her into his embrace. He wanted to comfort her. To alleviate her pain. He balled his hands into fists in his pockets, futilely trying to erase the desire to touch her.

She looked at him. "Don't you understand that you have treated me as nothing but an enemy when I had no *choice* in this," she stressed, splaying her hands, as she eyed him with eyes filled with the fire of her emotions. "I gave up so much of myself to do this for my father, and I *will not* fail him."

Alek nodded in understanding, turning from her as her confession struck a nerve about his own feelings of sacrifice and obligation. He moved to stand in front of her window seat. "I wanted to sail, to captain my own boat. To pave my own way in this world," he admitted with a little grunt. "My father and I were not getting along at the time of his death because of it. I, uh, could either accept the position or my father's shares would be sold and all proceeds donated to charity."

He'd never told that to anyone before. No one knew but his father's attorney and with so much ease, he handed Alessandra his biggest secret. It felt like a misstep.

"Oh, Alek," she sighed in compassion, coming over to stand beside him, and grabbed his arm as she looked up at him.

He looked down into her eyes and felt comforted by her understanding.

"You were forced into it, and Samira *wants* to be a part of the company—"

His body stiffened and he frowned deeply. "What do you know about my sister?" he asked, his tone hard.

"This weekend Samira asked for my help in gaining a position at ADG," she explained. "I looked at her résumé and I plan to help her, Alek."

He threw his hands up in exasperation. "Samira will not undermine my decision through you, and if she does I will cut her off," he said, feeling disrespected and annoyed.

Alessandra eyes widened in disbelief. "You *cannot* be that archaic, Alek. That closed-minded backward-ass thinking should *not* sit well with you," she spat, her ire matching his. "What do you have against women?"

"My issue is not all women, just unqualified ones," he shot back, and then felt small and petty. *Damn.*

"Unqualified," she said, standing in front of him to poke her finger into his chest.

"You must be out of your mind, *Captain Crunch*, when you just admitted you'd rather be sailing a doggone boat, but I and your sister with a Harvard degree and internships at some of the top companies in the world are unqualified?"

"Alessandra," he began, feeling regret.

"Alek, what kind of mess is that?" she asked, her face incredulous.

Again, the urge to comfort her filled him. "I spoke in anger about you and my sister," he confessed, as his eyes dropped to her mouth. "I can't think straight around you, Alessandra."

"Is that why you're so averse to women in the workplace, because you can't control your urges?" she asked him, moving to cross the room and pick up her wine goblet. "Well, bully for you, because I'm a woman who can control hers, and I don't date or screw anyone in the workplace. Not you or anyone else."

Alek eyed her standing there with one hand on her hip and one knee bent as she sipped from her wine, her chest heaving with her anger.

*Damn, she's sexy.*

"What?" she said, looking down at herself and then up at him in confusion.

The tension around them was thick and heady; passion and anger swirled in the air creating energy that pulsated against the walls of the house and their bodies.

He continued to stare, his eyes feasting on her. A tendril of hair escaping from her ponytail and caressing her neck. Even her bottom lip pressed against the glass. The fit of her tank on her full and high breasts. The high cut of her shorts, exposing her shapely thighs.

She squinted before her face filled with understanding. "No, Alek. No," she stressed.

"Your body says different," he said, taking in her nipples hardening and straining against the thin material.

She looked dismayed and covered her breasts with her forearm. "Go home, Alek," she said, quickly moving to the front door to open it wide.

"I will," he said, coming to stand before her. "But this thing between us will happen one day. I will make love to you, Alessandra, and we will enjoy it together."

She stepped back and felt the door, taking a deep swallow as she released a shaky breath.

She wanted him just as badly as he wanted her as he stepped close to her. It was hard to miss as she looked into his hot eyes. "It's better sooner than later so we can get it out of systems and focus on work, right? You're just as curious as I am. Will it be as good as we think?"

Alessandra's eyes dropped to his mouth and lingered there.

"Is curiosity killing that cat?" he taunted softly, his breath fanning against her mouth from their closeness.

She pouted before she released a little cry of alarm as she shifted her head to keep them from kissing.

He turned to stride away.

Alessandra reached out for him. "Yes, it is," she answered.

Alek turned and took one look at the surrender on her face. He pulled her body to his and kissed her passionately as he backed them into the house, closing the door behind them with one strong push.

# Chapter 7

*Am I crazy? Is this crazy? Should I stop it? I can't stop. I. Can't. Stop.*

"Just once," she pleaded in a whisper as Alek turned her around in his embrace and brought his hands up to slide beneath the hem of her shirt. His fingers softly trailed up her belly to stroke the underside of her breasts before palming them.

"Just once," he agreed.

She grunted in pleasure at the warmth of his touch as she let her head fall back against his chest and brought her hands up to stroke the back of his head. She shivered and cried out as he stroked her taut nipples with one hand before easing the other down to undo the button and zipper of her jean shorts. She arched her hips to shimmy her denims over her buttocks and down the length of her long legs.

"No panties?" he asked thickly.

She shook her head.

"Damn," Alek swore, easing his hand across the smooth and plump V of her core before he opened her moist outer lips with his middle finger to seek and find her clit.

Alessandra hissed between clenched teeth, her fingers briefly digging into his neck as she trembled.

"It's so wet," he moaned, pressing the fleshy bud between his forefinger and thumb as he eased his middle finger inside her.

Her body slackened against him as she gasped.

"Alessandra," Alek moaned in wonder.

She felt the length of him harden against her buttocks and rotated her hips, dragging her soft cheeks against him as she dropped her chin to her chest to look down at his hand buried between her thighs.

He pressed a sizzling kiss to her nape, licking her there before he sucked the same spot as his beard lightly tickled her.

"That feels good," she whimpered.

"What does?" he asked, bending his head to the side to look down at her face.

"Everything," she exhaled, opening her legs.

Alek followed her lead and slid his finger inside her more, until his knuckle rested on that small area between her core and buttocks. In and out. Circling against her walls. Then in and out again. And again. And again, even as he never stopped sliding her thick bud back and forth between his other fingers.

She ached. It was sweet torture. Her body craved release. Her senses said hold on for more.

He nodded against her hair, feeling the change in her. Her walls clutched and released his fingers. She got wetter. Hotter. She shivered nonstop.

He wanted it just as badly for her as she needed it for herself. "Come for me," he begged, his voice throaty from his own yearning. "Let me feel you come."

Alessandra closed her eyes and brought her hands up to squeeze and tease her own nipples as Alek lowered himself behind her to plant kisses to her lower back and softly bite the flesh of her buttocks. "I'm coming, Alek," she admitted with a whimper, her knees losing strength. "I'm coming for you."

He settled her buttocks on one shoulder to brace her as he continued to finger her to an explosive climax.

She thrust her hips forward against his hand as wave on top of wave of pleasure filled her. She floated. Her heart hammered. Her pulse raced. Her senses were on high alert. Her clit throbbed. She felt every bit of that white-hot explosion. It was pure bliss. "Yes. Yes. Yes," she cried out, the room fading to black.

Alek was persistent.

In and out. In and out. Again and again. And again. Fast. Hard. Pounding.

"No more," she cried out, thinking she might just lose her mind. She dropped her arms to try to push his hand away from her.

With a wolfish smile, he freed his finger, leaving a moist trail across her clean-shaven mound and then her belly as he wrapped his arm around her waist and stood to pick her shuddering body up against his.

Alek walked her over to the padded window bench

and sat her down on it. He quickly undressed with anxious, jerky movements before he spread her legs wide as he lowered himself to his knees. She leaned her head back against the wide railing and pressed a foot to each wall as she eyed him.

Amid the heat and passion, it was clear he appreciated the sight of her nudity. She completely lost her inhibitions as she lay before him. Ready for him. Still dealing with the aftereffects of coming for him. Hoping her body was everything he dreamed that she hid with her clothing.

"I'm aching for you, Alessandra," Alek said, the sight of her core open and wet for him, making his loins ache. "I can't wait any more to be inside you."

With heart pounding with so much force, Alek grabbed her ankles, locking her in place as he guided the smooth head of his steel inside her. She was tight. Wet. Hot. He barely gave her an inch before he stopped, afraid he would spill his seed too soon. He closed his eyes, seeking control.

Every nerve ending in his body seemed connected to electricity. There was a fine balance between pleasure and agony. It was maddening.

The moment his nut ebbed, Alek eased his hardness inside her, feeling her walls spread to allow him in. To fit him like a second skin. To grip him. Inch by inch until he filled her with it all.

She grimaced and bit her bottom lip with wide eyes as she waited for the discomfort to fade. "I feel it. I feel it. I feel it," she moaned with a whimper.

Alek's mouth formed into a circle as a small drizzle

of his release shot out against her walls. He freed her ankles and bent his body, loving the feel of her soft breasts against his chest as he kissed her as he began to stroke inside. Deeply. Slowly. Enjoying every moment. Every thrust.

The suspense was over. And being inside her was better than anything he could have ever dreamed.

"Alessandra," he moaned against her mouth before lightly biting the tip of her tongue.

Goose bumps raced across his skin as she stroked the sides of his face before trailing her fingertips down his neck, shoulders and arms with deliberate slowness that was addictive.

He eased back out of her, leaving just the tip resting at the throbbing opening of her femininity before he thrust his hips forward and filled her again, quickening his movements until he could outpace a piston.

She arched her back and broke their kiss to cry out in amorous abandon. "Alek," she gasped.

Alessandra stroked his bottom lip with her thumb, and he quickly turned his head to capture it in his mouth to suck deeply as he circled his hips, pressing his hard inches against her walls like he wanted to feel every possible spot inside her. He looked down at her, fueled by the hunger and pleasure on her face as he continued his onslaught. He had never felt so alive. So complete.

The moment just before a climax was the sweetest anticipation ever and Alek felt it coming on. Steady and strong. He wrapped his arms around her tightly, crushing her breasts against his chest as he captured her plush mouth with his own. She wrapped her legs around his buttocks and dug her fingers into the strength of his back as she rocked her hips in unison with him, causing her walls to pull down on his hardness and rush him toward his climax.

He felt it leave his hardness and coat her walls as he moaned with a wildness that only hinted at the dam that broke inside him. The spasmodic clutching and releasing of his tool by her silk walls, drained him.

They held each other tightly, as if afraid to release the other. As if the moment would fade or be found to be unreal.

Hours later, Alek eased the sheet off Alessandra's body, as she slept on her stomach in the middle of her king-size bed. He had awakened already hard for her, the lit lamp on her nightstand making his erection a long, curving shadow on the wall behind him. He wanted more of her.

He opened her legs and knelt between them, massaging the back of her thighs and buttocks before he bent to lick and lightly bite both soft round cheeks. Her skin was fresh and clean from their earlier shower. She awakened with a soft smile and a purr as Alek grabbed a pillow and lifted her up by the waist to shove it under her, causing her buttocks to arch higher in the air.

Alek licked his fingers and then stroked the tip of his erection to wet it before he gripped the thick base to guide it inside her from behind. He lay down flat atop her, loving the feel of her soft buttocks against him as he rocked inside her body.

Alessandra lifted her head from the pillow and clutched it with both her arms as she snaked her lower body, matching his powerful rhythm stroke for stroke.

He could only shake his head in wonder as he pressed kisses and tender bites from one brown shoulder to the other. "You ready?" he asked, his lips to her cheek.

She shook her head. "No, not yet."

Not wanting to leave her behind, Alek slid his hands beneath her soft body. With one he rolled her tight nipples between his fingers and with the other he teased her moist clit.

Alessandra bit down into the pillow with a grunt.

Using his chin, he moved her hair from her neck and buried his face there, sucking at that tender spot under her ear. "Now?" he asked, breathless as he continued to thrust inside her as she lay prone beneath him.

"Yes," she gasped.

Alek stroked her deeply, working hard with each thrust for his climax until his sweat coated both their bodies. He hollered out harshly as Alessandra clawed at the bed and muffled her own screams of release into her pillow.

Depleted, he rolled off her body. His chest heaving and his erection fading as he threw an arm over his eyes.

Soon their snores were as matched as their strokes.

As Alek slept, Alessandra sat on the opposite end of the bed and watched him. Broad shoulders. Toned arms. Hard chest. Chiseled abs. Long and thick hardness even at rest.

*Just beautiful. And sexy. And all mine...at least for the night.*

Soon the morning would come and their one night of passion would be over.

She rose from the bed and padded barefoot across the floor to her bathroom to make a sudsy washcloth. She carried it back into the bedroom, with a dry hand towel under her arm, uncaring that she left a wet trail on the wood floor.

Carefully she washed him.

Alek awakened with a start, looking up at her with wide eyes. "What are—"

"Sssssh," she said, holding a foam-covered finger to her mouth.

He relaxed his frame as she finished her task, smiling when he hardened in her hands.

Alessandra wiped away the suds with the dry cloth and flung it over her shoulder as she climbed on the bed, straddling his hips. Arching a brow, she squatted above him, holding his hardness straight with her hand as she eased down onto him.

She began her slow ride, sliding up and down the length of him as she looked at him with her hands pressed against his hard chest.

"Alessan—"

She pressed a hand to his mouth to quiet him, leaning down to replace her hand with her mouth. Their tongues lightly danced together as she worked nothing but her lower back and hips in a quick and steady pace that stoked that now-all-too-familiar fire. She broke their kiss to shift up enough to dangle her breasts above his mouth. Quickly he latched onto one and deeply sucked at her hard nipple, intensifying her pleasure as she felt her release rise. Cupping his head, she rode him fast and hard until she felt him stiffen inside her before his release filled her. With a cry she couldn't contain, Alessandra brought her core up and down his shaft as she came with him.

Trembling and shaken, they held each other tightly as she rode him until he went soft inside.

"Damn," they swore in unison before they both laughed.

Late into the night, Alessandra and Alek slept in her bed, their limbs entwined as if feeding a simple need to know the other was still there. Their passion for each other seemed limitless. Both had lost count of just how many times they mated. At times, it was slow and passion-filled. Other times, fierce and fast. Each time, they were completely lost in each other. Inhibitions released. Passion reigned.

Sleep was their only respite.

Alek was the first to rise the next morning. He didn't awaken Alessandra as she slept with a pillow snuggled beneath her upper body. He didn't dare believe he would be able to walk away from her if she even looked at him. As he got dressed he watched her, missing not one detail.

Her mussed hair, long since freed of her ponytail. The way she slept with her mouth slightly ajar. The love bite on her shoulder. The curve of her body under the sheet as she lay on her side. One brown nipple peeking from under the sheet to tempt him.

*I better go now.*

He carried his shoes and moved around the bed, pausing long enough to press a warm kiss to her lower back—a spot he discovered was one of her erogenous zones. With one last glance over his shoulder, he left her bedroom, quietly closing the door behind him. He slid on his shoes and left her house, still perplexed that she chose to live in the guesthouse and give free run of her mansion to her family.

He was fast discovering that she was a woman of complexities.

Alek stood there outside her house with his hand pressed to the door. He dropped his head and wiped his hand over his beard as he desperately fought the urge to retrace his steps and climb back in Alessandra's bed.

Alek gripped the doorknob for long, torturous moments before finally releasing it and climbing into his glossy dark blue Bugatti Chiron. As he reversed the car and then turned forward to accelerate the sports car up the drive, leaving her felt like one of the toughest things he ever had to do. Last night with her had created a hunger in him that he doubted any other woman could satisfy.

*Just once?*

He shook his head at their naïveté.

Alek looked ahead at the mansion framed by the blue, lavender and streaks of orange in the sky as the sun inched its way to prominence. In the distance, he spotted a male figure hurrying down the steps leading from a wrought iron balcony wearing nothing but a robe. Frowning, he slowed down. "Is that Victor?" he asked aloud.

He eased forward enough to watch as the older man scurried across the back lawn to a small stone home that he vaguely remembered as the servants' quarters from visiting the estate decades ago with his family. The front door opened and a young woman dressed only in a short nightie smiled up at him as he reached her. "That slick old bastard," he said.

He sped away, driving under the carport and eventually down the paved drive until he reached the security gate. He lowered the window to show his face to the monitor. If the system were anything like his own security, it was just as important knowing who exited the estate as it was to know who was entering.

Seconds, later the gates opened.

"Have a good day, Mr. Ansah," one of the guards' voices came crystal clear through the intercom.

Alek nodded and raised the window as he sped forward.

As he drove through the serene streets of Passion Grove, Alek had to admit there was something charming about the small town even in the wee hours of the morning before daylight. The town was a well-known secret for those with big dollars seeking a small-town setting. Still, his lifestyle moved at a faster pace and he enjoyed his penthouse apartment in Tribeca. Everything about Passion Grove spoke of family and settling down, even if it was still in the lap of luxury.

He wasn't ready yet.

He slowed down when he spotted the lit window of one of the businesses under the row of black canopies. *La Boulangerie* was etched on the door. It was French for bakery. His stomach grumbled and he lowered the window to inhale the scent of fresh baked goods and coffee that filled the air. He immediately pulled the car into a parking spot on the brick-paved road and climbed out to jog across the street.

Alek entered and felt like he was in an old-world pastry shop from Europe with its brick walls, wood beams, polished hardwood floors, metal accents, and black bistro tables and chairs. He wasn't surprised. Passion Grove was a small town with big-time character.

A tall man with a blond man-bun, who looked more like a sun-kissed California surfer than a man from the East Coast, came from the rear of the bakery. His black apron was embroidered in white with *Bill the Pâtissier*. "Sorry, we're not open for a couple hours. Just getting some baking done," he said, his accent decidedly Jersey.

Alek nodded in understanding, but his stomach protested. "Listen, I have a little ride to Tribeca ahead of me and I am starving," he said. "I will purchase whatever you have that's done and a cup of coffee."

Bill smiled and shrugged. "I feel you, bro," he said. "Nothing fresh is ready yet, but I do have some petits fours left from yesterday."

Alek gave him a small mock bow. "My forever gratitude."

"Your English accent is awesome, bro," he said as he filled a black paper cup with coffee from one of six French press coffee makers lining the counter.

Alek chuckled. "Yours, as well," he mused.

The laid-back baker pressed a lid on the cup and handed it to him over the butcher-block counter before turning to walk through a black swinging door.

Alek tasted the coffee. His face filled with surprise as he sipped again. He looked up at the sound of a chuckle.

The baker set a tray of a variety of petits fours on the counter. "Coffee's good, right?" he asked with confidence.

"*Damn* good," Alek stressed, taking another deep sip as he stepped forward to eye the tray of treats.

"The secret is all in the beans, the right farmer with the right packaging of the right arabica bean," Bill boasted, reaching for a small box under the counter.

"Do you know Alessandra Dalmount?" Alek asked, his thoughts returning to her.

The baker looked incredulous. "Of *course*, bro," he said. "As a matter of fact, she loves these citrus petits fours glacés."

Alek envisioned her tucking one of the small square treats in her mouth. "Let me get all of those, too," he said, reaching in his back pocket for his billfold, pulling out his American Express Centurion card.

"Sorry, dude, I haven't turned on my register yet," Bill said. "Listen, the coffee and petits fours are on the house. Enjoy."

"Wow. Thank you," he said, replacing his card.

"No problem," he said, handing over a large black pastry bag.

Alek pulled five hundred-dollar bills from the wallet and folded them to slide into a glass carafe on the counter. "Consider this a tip, then," he said, before turning to walk out of the bakery.

He chuckled at Bill's exclamation from behind him.

Once back behind the wheel of his sports car with the box of pastries safely on the passenger seat, Alek settled in and enjoyed the feel of driving as he made his way back to lower Manhattan. With a yawn that spoke to the lack of real sleep he had gotten last night, he enjoyed the taste of the coffee and welcomed any energy it gave him. He rarely drove because it was such an inconvenience in the city, but he welcomed the feel of handling the sports car. It was almost as smooth a ride as Alessandra.

His gut clenched as he glanced at the pastry box. He planned to leave the box of treats on her desk as a surprise, but outside of that he didn't know where they went from there. How would they interact? Would it be awkward?

And businesswise, would she expect him to change his views on her place in the business after last night? Because he hadn't. Would that anger her?

Alek released a heavy breath.

As much as he enjoyed last night, as much as he craved being with her again, Alek was fast realizing that he had just made things far too complicated.

Once she heard the front door close and the roar of the engine of Alek's car, Alessandra opened her eyes and stopped feigning sleep. She hadn't been ready to face Alek just yet. That would come later. She rolled over to the side where he had slept and pressed her face into his pillow. His scent lingered, and she inhaled deeply of it.

*Last night was magnificent.*

One time with Alek Ansah had done anything *but* get him out of her system.

Alessandra climbed from the bed, wincing at the tenderness between her thighs as she walked across the long expanse of the bedroom to her en suite bathroom. She took a shower, enjoying the feel of the massive rainfall showerhead pouring down on her while the heads on the walls pulsed against her body. Once done, she made sure the glass door was sealed tight and pressed the digital button to fill the oversize stall with steam. She took a seat on the marble-tiled bench, leaning back against the wall as she awaited her own type of therapy. Soon eucalyptus-scented steam swirled around her until it was thick as clouds.

What she usually saw as just calming had become erotic last night as Alek bent her over the bench and stroked her from behind as the steam caressed their bodies.

His imprint was now on her entire house. No place was free of a steamy recollection of him.

Aware of the time, Alessandra wrapped a towel around her damp body and left the shower. She quickly dressed in leggings and a baggy T-shirt before driving her golf cart up to the main house. Victor was lounging by the pool with a satisfied smile on his face as he smoked a cigar.

"See you in the office today, Victor?" she called over to him as she passed.

He laughed like she'd told a Kevin Hart–level joke.

"Of course not," she said drily, speeding ahead.

Alessandra parked by the stone water feature and jogged up the steps to walk in through one of the towering double doors of the front entry. The lights of the chandelier high above in the entrance hall were dimmed. The quiet was unusual. As she picked up a stack of mail from the table in the center of the round foyer, she paused to smell the fresh flowers arranged in a tall vase atop it.

She smiled up at the massive painting of her parents on the wall as she tucked the mail under her arm and crossed the tiled floor to the elevator. The ride up to the third floor was brief. She passed the double doors leading into her master suite and instead went to the room at the end of the west wing. Her hairstylist would arrive at six as she did every Monday morning to do Alessandra's hair for the week in her home salon.

She picked up the phone and dialed the kitchen, "Good morning, Olga," she said. "Breakfast for two, please, and I would love some pancakes."

Olga, the estate's house manager of the last twenty years, chuckled warmly. "With or without walnuts?" she asked.

Alessandra smiled. "With," she insisted, using a finger to push the styling chair. It circled.

"I missed you at dinner last night," she said. "Chef made roast pork. Your favorite."

"I wasn't up for the peanut gallery last night," she said with a shake of her head as she turned to play with her hair in the mirror.

"Are you ever?"

"No," she stressed.

"I'll bring the plates up so I can see you before you're gone for the week."

"Thank you."

She hung up the phone and leaned against the rear of the chair as she continued to study her reflection. *Do I look different because I feel different?*

"Here you are."

Alessandra turned to smile at her aunt Leonora. The silver-haired woman with freckled skin the color of shortbread was in a floor-length satin robe with an unlit cigarette in one hand and in the other, a champagne flute of orange juice that undoubtedly was a mimosa with more Veuve Clicquot than anything else. "I saw you drive up and wondered where you'd gotten to in this goliath we call home."

"Getting my hair done for the week ahead," she explained, taking a seat in the chair.

Leonora nodded, taking a sip and eyeing her niece's hair over the rim of the crystal. "I know hair messed up during sex when I see it. *That's* a sweat out," she said, running the tip of her tongue over her teeth. "Good for you."

Alessandra grimaced as she reached up to smooth the wildness from her mane.

"Alek has a strong African back and good abs—it should have been a-maz-ing," she drawled with a wink. "Right?"

"Wrong," she insisted, rotating the chair to avoid her aunt's all-too-knowing eyes.

"Oh no," Leonora sighed, wiggling her pinkie finger at Alessandra with a question in her eyes.

*Definitely not.*

"Aunt Leonora, didn't you attend finishing school?" she asked.

"Yes, I finished off everything they taught me with my love of a good dirty martini," she said, taking a deep sip of her drink with a satisfying—and completely unruly—smack of her lips.

Alessandra hid a smile behind her hand. Leonora had moved to Passion Grove from her villa in Paris—and a lover twenty years her junior—when Alessandra's mother passed away. She took on raising her niece, and for that Alessandra was loyal to her and endlessly forgiving of her lack of tact.

"You deserve love, my beautiful niece," Leonora said in a rare moment of seriousness as she came over to lightly stroke Alessandra's chin. Her eyes became bright. "The kind of love your parents had for each other. I never had that."

Alessandra's heart tugged at her aunt's hint of a sad smile and the tears brimming in her wide-set eyes.

"I want that for you. A lifetime without love—real love—is not easy. Please believe me," she pleaded, her voice barely above a whisper.

Alessandra rose to pull her thin frame into a tight embrace. "Aunt Leonora, I'm okay," she lied.

She was far from okay. At times her loneliness was draining, but with her busy life of tackling the business world, keeping up with her demanding family and carving out a few hours for herself, Alessandra didn't have the time or inclination to date. Last night with Alek had been her first passionate rendezvous in nearly two years. She was so driven to prove her detractors wrong that she felt dating or a relationship would diminish her focus.

And love?

That was weakness and a gateway to heartbreak.

Leonora's body began to quiver, and Alessandra rolled her eyes heavenward as she shook her head. "What, Auntie?" she asked, knowing the moment of deep reflection had passed.

"I *know* you're okay this morning after the night you had," she said, barely getting it out between her bawdy giggles.

Alessandra hugged her tighter and pressed a kiss to her smooth cheek as she reached down to lightly swat her buttocks in playful reprimand.

"Gave you some of the good ole African loving that had you thinking drums was playing in the background," she joked.

Alessandra leaned back and smiled down at her. "I love you, Aunt Lenora," she said. "See, I do have love in my life."

"As long as I'm alive and even after I'm gone, Allie," she promised, going back to her childhood nickname for her. "Just make sure that's enough."

"Okay," Alessandra agreed, wondering if it was.

# *Chapter 8*

*Two weeks later*

Alessandra dropped her Aurora pen atop the feasibility studies for each of the subsidiaries under the ADG umbrella. She sat her chin in her palm as she looked over at the secret doorway behind the bookcase that led to the passageway between her office and Alek's. She bit her bottom lip, glancing down at the report and then back at the door as she stroked the back of her tight topknot.

The first time she used it had also been the last.

*Is it still locked?*

She leaned back in her chair and clasped her hands in her lap as she crossed her legs in the acid-green printed crepe de chine Valentino dress she wore, causing the kick pleats at the hem to open and expose black silk. For the last two weeks, it had been business as usual between them. Business meetings. Corporate luncheons. Cordiality. Distance. Pretense.

Like *it* never happened.

Alessandra lightly stroked her throat with the tips of her black-coated fingernails, turning from the hidden portal. She was an actress. Being around Alek and keeping herself from staring at him, touching him, or pretending her heart was not racing with the speed of one of his sports cars was a Viola Davis–level brilliant performance.

Was he giving a tour de force performance as well, or had that one night been enough?

*If so, what were the petits fours about?*

She had found them on her desk that morning, immediately recognizing the box from the bakery back home in Passion Grove. Through the day she had devoured the six citrus petits fours. Licking her lips, she opened the top drawer of her desk and withdrew the card that had been attached to the box. "Your fave, huh? Now I know another one of your secrets, Alessandra," she read. "Enjoy them slowly like I did my sweet treat last night. A."

She tilted her head back at the hot memory of him tongue-kissing her down below that night two weeks ago. Her climax had been achingly slow and completely mind-wrecking.

"Whooooooo," Alessandra breathed, as her tiny bud pulsed with new life.

She'd thought she wasn't going to ever stop climaxing.

"Alessandra," she admonished herself, picking up her pen and forcing her attention away from memories of Alek stroking deep inside her to the reports on her desk.

And then there was the elephant that stayed posted up in any room both she and Alek were in. The next board meeting was in two weeks and they were expected to make the decision on who would concede on their acquisition plan. They had yet to discuss it since the board meeting during the Jubilee weekend. She pushed aside the report and reached down to pick up the bright red hardcover folder holding Alek's report, sitting it in her lap and rotating in her chair to face the bright light of the window. She squinted in concentration, lightly biting the tip of her nail, as she read through the entire report for what had to be the third time in the past two weeks. This time when she was done she went back to the beginning and read it again.

She closed the folder and lightly drummed her fingernails against the top of it as she looked out window, lost in thought. His choice of airline to acquire was solid. All his reports substantiated his selection. The stocks were priced aggressively, making it an ideal time to acquire those necessary to gain majority ownership and have less risk of a low return. His market research showed an upsurge in the viability of the airline industry. He even researched the current executives in place to ensure that keeping them in their current position would ease the transition period.

She was willing to admit his venture was a better acquisition for ADG.

"But *something* is nagging at me," she whispered aloud.

*Think. Think. Think. Think.*

"Come on, Alessandra. What is it?"

*Bzzzzzz.*

"Damn," she swore, her chain of thought broken.

Alessandra whirled around in the chair with the velocity of the cartoon Tasmanian Devil. She hit the intercom button on her conference phone. "Yes, Unger," she said forcing civility into her tone when she felt like being belligerent.

"I don't have any lunch plans on your schedule and I wondered if you wanted to order in?" he asked.

She glanced down at her watch. Three hours had passed. "Um, yes, I'll be staying in," she said, searching for clarity. "Um, I'll have my usual from that sandwich place."

"Pisillio," he offered. "I'll go get it. I have a coupon."

Alessandra arched a brow. "A coupon?" she balked. "Unger, just use the card I gave you for expenses."

"I am, but a deal is a deal," he said. "Why pay more for something if you don't have to?"

"Right. Thanks, Unger." She removed her finger from the button and sat the folder atop all the paperwork on her desk.

*Okay, where was I? Think. Think. Think. Think.*

She rose from her seat and began pacing the length of her office, her heels echoing against the hardwood floors.

*Tap-tap-tap-tap-tap...tap...tap...tap.*

Alessandra came to a stop with her hands outstretched and her eyed closed. "I got it," she said, rushing back over to her desk and quickly flipping through the pages of the proposal until she reached the financial sections. "Thank you, Unger."

When her lunch arrived, Alessandra used one hand

to flip through and search sites on her touch screen computer and with the other she held her delicious panini of Parmacotto ham and fresh mozzarella with tomatoes, arugula and lemon dressing on fresh-baked bread. She was a dog on the hunt and her entire body tingled, letting her know she was close to her prey.

It was late afternoon when she finally dropped her pen and rubbed her eyes. She laughed a little as she looked down at the proposal with red slashings and notes in the margin. She felt exhilarated. It was such moments that she felt business was in her blood, and maybe—just maybe—her father had seen it in her.

*And now maybe Alek will, as well.*

Alek closed his eyes as he lay on the low-slung bright red sofa in the lounge area of his office. Jay-Z's song "4:44" played from the wireless speakers and he was lost in the music and the words. He needed a break from the world, and for him, music offered that.

As the jazz-influenced beat swelled in the air, he had an image of Alessandra flinging her head back and laughing before she smiled with a carefree and pleased look in her beautiful brown eyes.

In the last two weeks, he'd seen her nearly every day and still he missed her. There had been a shift after that night. A subtle change that maybe no one else noticed, but he had. Even as they avoided each other's eyes and made sure to never be alone with each other, his desire to just be in her atmosphere had intensified. The need to berate, embarrass or lessen had faded. Most moments of the day he wanted nothing more than to see her smile, and all moments of the night he wanted a replay of *that* night.

The scent of her hair and her neck and her femininity haunted him.

The discovery that she was far more than even his dreams captivated him.

The struggle not to stride in her office and press her body to the floor tortured him.

He sat up and swiped his finger across the tablet to end the music abruptly.

Still the opening refrain played in his head, nagging at him and speaking to his life.

He rose to slide his hands in his pockets and walk over to stand at the windows lining his office. Was he running the way he accused her? Definitely. He had never wanted to just be with a woman the way his mind and his body craved Alessandra.

That didn't sit well with him. That feeling was a doorway to emotions he didn't want to allow.

He shrugged and shook his head as his focus became his refection and not the sky-reaching buildings before him. His office door opened behind him and he shifted his eyes to the right to see Alessandra standing in the doorway. His body stiffened and his heart double-pumped as he licked his lips and freed one of his hands to stroke his bearded chin. And just like that, with the sudden appearance of her in his space, he felt rejuvenated…and if he was honest with himself, also nervous and unsure. That was unfamiliar territory.

"Hello, Alessandra," Alek said as he turned to face her as she strolled in with the hem of her skirt swaying back and forth across the thickest part of her thighs.

She stopped before his desk and held a large red binder against her chest. Her eyes shifted to the hidden door of the secret passageway.

He looked at it and then back at her before he walked over to release the latch locking it. "How can I help you?" he asked, coming back to take a seat behind his desk.

"You win," she said, setting the wide binder on his desk and opening it to a certain page.

He recognized his proposal. "Win what?" he asked, frowning at the sight of her bright red markings on the pages.

"I agree that we go forward with your proposal and not mine," she said.

Alek was surprised and he didn't bother to hide it. "That really was one helluva night, wasn't it?" he quipped, and then instantly regretted it. Nothing but male bravado and his uncertainty about their relationship brought it on.

Alessandra's face tightened in annoyance. "Your immature ego is exactly why I don't normally mix business with pleasure," she said, her voice ice-cold.

He nodded. "My apologies. That was childish, Alessandra, and I'm sorry," he said, looking up to lock his eyes with hers, hoping she saw his sincerity in the depths.

Her body relaxed. "I came in to talk business and how I have a discovered a way to improve an already solid deal and save ADG another million dollars during the acquisition," she said, coming around the desk to lean over him a bit to press her fingertips to the page.

The scent of her perfume, with its warm citrus notes, surrounded him. He leaned back a bit to look down the length of her legs, and his palms itched to stroke the softness of the back of her knees.

"Really, Alek," she said.

He shifted his eyes up from her legs to find her looking back over her shoulder at him. "'I can resist everything except temptation,'" he quoted, as he waved a hand by way of asking her to remove the enticement.

"Oscar Wilde," she said, moving around the desk to take a seat in one of the black club chairs before it.

"I am a fan of the playwright," he admitted.

"As am I," she said, crossing her legs.

His eyes dipped to take in the move.

Alessandra sighed and uncrossed them, leaning forward to tap the proposal. "Focus, Alek," she said.

He pulled the binder closer and began to seriously consider her revisions. With every passing moment, his brows dipped into a frown. He looked up at her before double-checking her facts, figures and notes. "So, we would be able to purchase the stock directly from them at a savings of a little over a million," he said.

"Why pay more for something if you don't have to?" she said with one shoulder shrug.

"And you discovered this on your own?" he asked, shocked that she discovered something he and his team had missed.

Alessandra threw her hands up in exasperation. "Alek, seriously. Come on," she moaned.

He leaned back in his chair and eyed her. He knew in that moment that it was time for him to concede, as well. Alessandra Dalmount had just finessed an already strong deal and deserved respect for that.

"Alek, it is time to put aside your resistance and your ego to accept that we can make ADG more successful as a team—the same way our fathers joined forces and worked together to start the company," she said, sitting on the edge of the chair and not at all hiding her passion and conviction. “If we just take our focus and energy off the constant battles with each other, then we could both do our jobs better.”

Alek remained silent.

Alessandra stood. “I truly would love to end the war between us, Alek,” she said before she turned to take her leave.

He hurried across the office, reaching out to catch her arm before she opened the door, turning her body and pressing her against it with his own. The flutter of her lashes and the quickness of her breath from their closeness was revealing. “Love conquers war,” he stated in a low voice.

“We don’t love each other,” she countered, her eyes dropping to his mouth.

“No, but we want each other, and that’s close enough,” Alek said as he lowered his head to hers.

Her resistance was weak at best. She breathed his name into his mouth in that second just before he kissed her. Her body went soft against his as she snaked her hands up around his neck to splay her hands on the back of his head.

Alek’s heart felt like it was fueled with pure adrenaline as he pressed his hands between her body and the door to raise her hem and cup her soft buttocks. He swallowed her gasp of pleasure as he lifted her up against the door and pressed his hips against her so that she could feel his aching hardness. Being there with her, caught up in their heat, kissing with a passion that was a feast after a famine was intoxicating.

*Bzzzzzz...*

The intercom broke through their haze.

Alessandra ended the kiss, tilting her head back against the door as she shook her head.

"No, no, no," he pleaded, leaning in to lightly bite her chin.

Alessandra pressed her hands against his shoulders, still shaking her head, as she dropped down to her feet. She glanced at him briefly as she corrected the fit of her black lace panties before she smoothed her skirt down. "Business always comes first, Alek. Our fathers didn't put us in charge just to sex each other in the office," she said, her voice shaky as she walked unsteadily to the door leading to their private hall.

*Bzzzzzz...*

He stood there with his erection straining against his zipper, watching her leave, and already felt the loss of her. "Thank you for your help, Alessandra," he said. "You proved me wrong."

She turned and leaned against the door as she looked at him in surprise.

"Promise me we will have dinner tonight to celebrate our teamwork on this deal?" he asked, his heart pounding as he watched her closely.

Alessandra said nothing and just nodded as she licked her lips before turning to leave him.

Hours later, long after night reigned, Alessandra lightly bit the side of her finger as she watched Alek easily steering his Bugatti. He was looking ahead, focused on the road, and she allowed herself to enjoy his profile. His beautiful brown skin all the more flawless by his faded haircut and his groomed beard that couldn't shield the square cut of his jaw. Long lashes that resembled small wings whenever he blinked. Supple mouth. Beautiful.

He glanced over the small divide between them, catching her eyes resting on him, and he smiled.

Alessandra looked away, her nervousness causing her teeth to dip a little deeper into the flesh of her finger.

"We're here," Alek said, driving through the entrance to a marina.

"I thought we were just having dinner?" she asked, her eyes taking in the sights of the boats and yachts lining the docks with the lit Lower Manhattan highrises in the distance as he pulled into an assigned parking spot.

"Don't worry," he said, opening the car door. "I'm going to feed you."

She waited as he came around the front of the sports car and opened her door for her. Taking his hand, she left the car and inhaled of the scent of the river. She walked beside him, quiet but curious, as they made their way down the dock to a sixty-foot white motor yacht.

Alessandra smiled at *LuLu's Baby* inscribed in gold-trimmed turquoise lettering on the bow. "This is pretty humble for you, Mr. Bugatti," she teased. "I wouldn't have expected that."

She pointed to a sleek all-black mega yacht of close to two hundred feet docked on the other side of the marina.

He chuckled. "That's *Black Joy* and it is mine as well, Alessandra."

Her nod was smug. "Of course."

"We're having dinner on *LuLu's Baby* because it requires less crew," he explained.

"How many?" she asked as she looked up at a tall, stout man with skin as brown as chocolate coming out of the covered main level of the vessel.

Alek gave her a wide smile. "Me," he said. "And that's the chef."

Alessandra glanced at the boat and then back at him. "So you never really let go of your dreams of sailing?" she asked.

A warm breeze blew in from the river as he looked up at the yacht with his anticipation clear. "It's not in the way that I wanted, but it knocks the edge off the hunger."

His eagerness was childlike and infectious.

"Permission to board, Captain Ansah?" she asked playfully, fighting the urge to kiss his cheek.

He waved his hand with a nod of his head.

Together they boarded. Alek introduced her to Chef Justice Brown, a Michelin-starred chef and winner of a James Beard Award, before Alessandra removed her heels. She already knew it was yacht etiquette not to wear street shoes on board and slipped on brand-new flip-flop sandals sitting in a basket. He led her up to the aft deck.

As he removed his suit jacket he stood in the helm station and began pushing buttons on the panel to start the engine. Alessandra moved to stand at the railing as a soft summer breeze blew in from the river again and fluttered a tendril of her hair that loosened from her topknot. "I would have gone home and changed or had my stylist bring me something if I knew you were planning all of this," she said, looking down at the marina's dockhands working fast to cast off the lines securing the vessel to the dock.

"Actually, I called Shiva myself and you have a change of clothes on board," he said with a mischievous glint in his eye as he slowly shifted into forward at idle speed.

"And?" she asked, just as the yacht began to pull away from the dock.

He focused on keeping the yacht clear of any other boats, looking handsome sans tie and jacket with the top buttons of his custom shirt undone. "*And* there's an outfit for tomorrow—"

"Tomorrow!" she exclaimed, her eyes widened by shock.

Alek cast her a charming smile that was all white teeth and bright eyes. "I thought we were celebrating our new alliance," he said.

"A night on a yacht is more about the pleasure you seek than the business, Alek," she said, hating that his charm softened her tone. "And we agreed it was just that one night, remember?"

He opened his mouth.

She shook her head. "Today in your office didn't change that for me, Alek," she insisted. "So why play with fire?"

As the boat entered free and clear water, Alek gradually increased the speed until soon the wind whipped across their bodies. "You have your own cabin and tomorrow I want to take us to my family's private island off East Hampton."

Alessandra was reluctant. "'I can resist everything except temptation,'" she reminded him.

"I promise to be on my best behavior," Alek said, watching her closely.

She smiled. "That's what I'm worried about," she mused.

They shared a laugh filled with the all-too-familiar sexual tension pulsing between them.

"To resisting temptation," he said.

She said nothing as she looked out at the moon's reflection on the water.

"Today was amazing, Alek. Thank you for sharing your island with me."

He glanced back at her from behind the aviator shades he wore to block some of the sun's rays. They were lounging on the bi-level deck that connected to the dock and enjoying the view of the river vista with the bright blue skies only broken up with clouds of varying thickness. She looked beautiful with her hair undone from her topknot, pulled back off her face and the bottom half loosened and floating down just past her shoulders in a white off-the-shoulder crochet cover she wore atop a white strapless bikini. "You're welcome," he said, forcing himself to look away as he sat on the dock with the legs of his white linen pants folded up to have his feet in the water.

As they had explored the abandoned camp in the midst of the towering pine trees, Alek told her of his plans to create a North American vacation spot for his family and the generations to come complete with a landing strip to enjoy entry to the island retreat by private airplane. He was going to clear it all except the surrounding acreage protected by a conservation easement and build a new dock close enough to the estate to walk out of the house and down one flight of steps to reach it.

He had enjoyed sharing his vision with her and loved the suggestions she made. She truly was smart and innovative, with a sharp wit that had him laughing several times throughout the day.

He looked back at her again, swatting away some flying insect that landed against his bare, sweat-soaked chest to find her eyes on him. She looked away as if caught doing something wrong. His eyes dipped to take in her long, shapely legs where she lay on a blanket he brought to enjoy their picnic lunch.

Last night, after he dropped anchor in the middle of the river, they'd enjoyed their dinner of roasted lamb shoulder in the main salon and successfully resisted that familiar buzz of awareness they created around each other. Afterward they sipped champagne and lounged on the deck stargazing. Neither said much, but the night air around them was bursting with tension and temptation.

Long after they retired to their separate staterooms, Alek had lain naked atop the covers on his king-size bed fighting his desire to go to her. Alessandra wanted him just as badly as he wanted her, that he knew. He was confident a knock at her door would lead to another explosive night.

But he refrained. It had been a true test of his will.

He took in the curves of her body with a regret-filled shake of his head.

That resolve was fading fast.

"I'm not blind, Alek," she said, sitting up with her arms braced against the desk. "Is that too much? Me and you being here...alone?"

He smiled and focused his eyes on the yacht sitting moored to the dock. "Honestly, it is," he admitted. "I want nothing more than to come over and give you what we *both* want, Alessandra."

She rose and came over to sit on the dock beside him. "What do you want from me, Alek?" she asked. "If I admit that I would surprise you with how wet I am from just looking at you, then what? Because I'm not looking for love or a relationship, and sex could complicate things with ADG, don't you think?"

He removed his shades and looked into her eyes, seeing the question, the concern and the hesitance. "I can't put what we shared behind me, and I don't want to, Alessandra," he confessed, heart pounding.

Her eyes warmed over and she brought her hand up to cup the back of his neck as she leaned in to touch her forehead to his. "I crave you," she admitted, her words softly whispering against his mouth.

"Just once more," he said, his body alive with hope and want.

"We said that the last time," she reminded him with a teasing smile before she brought her hand up to his chest and stroked the fine, flat hairs there as she tilted her chin up to taste his full mouth with her own.

He grunted in pleasure, pulling her pliant body over to straddle his lap as he removed the cover-up that did its job far too well.

They gave in to that craving yet again with nothing but surrounding flora to tell. They were witnesses to their passion. The rays of the sun and their slow, deliberate exertion caused sweat to coat their brown skin, slickening the primal movements against each other. And when they reached their climax together, their wild cries of release and fulfillment blended in the air above, echoing for miles.

Afterward, as they lay there seeking control of their bodies again, Alessandra breathlessly asked, "This wasn't the last time, was it?"

"Hell no," Alek swore.

# *Chapter 9*

*Three months later*

It was only late October but the northeastern chill was present, the type of wintry air you feel in your bones. The type of cold to make you thankful for a warm body to press up against. To yearn to be close to.

*Thank God it's Friday.*

Alessandra stretched her arms wide across the smooth leather of the back of the Jaguar with a smile on her face almost as wide. The week was over and Passion Grove was her destination, but lately her weekends at home had found new meaning. She thought of that song "The Weekend" by R & B soulstress SZA.

As the lyric played in her head, she smiled and let her head fall back against the seat. Monday through Friday she and Alek were all business, but their weekends in her little guesthouse in Passion Grove were all about each other, their escape from hiding their liaisons from the world.

Alek had agreed to her request to not reveal their affair because of her fear she would lose her respect in the industry—something she worked so hard to attain and maintain. They even went so far as publicly dating other people at work functions—with the stipulation that the dates went no further than just that. Sex with anyone else was completely off the table.

She remembered the late-summer party they held on the terrace of their office building to celebrate the acquisition and ADG's shift into the airline industry with his brother Naim being named the president. She'd brought Hill and he had his standard model type floating beside him when he entered. All night they surreptitiously watched each other until the party was over. In the end, it was all foreplay because they both sent their dates home before hotly pleasing each other atop the conference table in their boardroom.

As Roje drove up to the guesthouse on her estate, her heart skipped a beat to see that the windows of her living room were bright with light. She hadn't left them on when she left on Monday and her cleaning staff wouldn't have done so. Quickly, she eased her underwear over her hips and down the length of her legs and her heels to shove inside her purse. "Enjoy your weekend, Roje," she said, climbing from the rear before he could exit.

"Yes, ma'am," he said,

Alessandra held the edges of her bright yellow Maki Oh robe coat closer as she hurried inside the house. She moaned in satisfaction at the feel of the heat as she pulled off her coat and eyed Alek sitting atop the plush rug before the fire, already naked and waiting. She dropped her handbag and briefcase on the sofa as she walked over to him and hitched the leather eyelet hem of her fitted black dress up around her waist as she stood over him.

"You beat me here," she said.

"That damn dress drove me crazy all day," he said, leaning in to lightly bite her plump mound before he pulled her down onto his lap and kissed her with every bit of the hunger he felt.

It was just what she needed.

Monday through Friday they were married to their business, but on Saturday and Sunday?

The weekend was all about getting lose in each other.

"Are you sure you want to do this?"

Alek dug his hands deeper into the pockets of his wool jacket and looked at the lengthy line of people waiting before he answered Alessandra's question. "Yeah," he said, his reluctance obvious.

She laughed as she tucked one of her hands in his pocket and entwined her cold fingers with his.

He looked down at her with her shades and a navy skullcap on over her now-waist-length hair in a long braid over one shoulder. *She's adorable*, he thought, loving the casual look of her navy peacoat, jeans and caramel riding boats as they shifted forward with the crowd awaiting entrance to the annual harvest festival held by Passion Grove's local orchard.

Nearly every resident of the small town had to be in attendance, plus those from neighboring cities. When she lightly hinted that she hadn't missed the annual festival celebrating the fall season since she was a kid, he had set aside his reluctance and offered to go.

Hayrides, apple bobbing and pumpkin carving were out of character for his jet-set lifestyle, but making Alessandra happy had become his favorite pastime. So they were both in skullies and shades—their idea of incognito—preparing to enjoy a day of fall frivolity.

Alek felt his iPhone vibrating against his buttocks in the back pocket of his distressed denims. He pulled it out and smiled at Chance's name, quickly answering. "What's up, Mr. Castillo?" he asked.

Alessandra gave him a wide stare and held a finger to her bare mouth. He nodded, assuring her that he wouldn't reveal his location to a man she'd discovered was his best friend and confidant.

"Well, hi, stranger. What do you have going on today?" Chance asked. "Helena needs a break from the cold and we're jetting to my place in Cabrera. You in?"

Alek thought about relaxing in the warmth on the terrace of his friend's palatial estate in the small and beautiful town in the Dominican Republic. "You won't believe where I am right now," he drawled, hardly believing it himself as the gates to the orchard opened and the small crowd swelled. Alessandra pulled him by the arm to a stand selling apple cider.

"Where's that, amigo?"

"A fall festival," he said, looking around at the line of booths and the elaborate fall decor that he had to admit was warm and inviting. Children were in line to have their faces painted by someone in a pumpkin costume. Booths offering different fall-centered treats were selling their goodies. In the distance, a band was playing upbeat music from a stage next to a line of food trucks and picnic tables. People were already picking pumpkins from the large crates on display.

Chance laughed. "No way."

Alek nodded as he accepted the cup Alessandra handed him before she tore off a piece of pastry and slid it into his mouth.

"Apple turnover. Good, right?" she asked, before enjoying a bite of the treat herself and then licking the sweet glaze from her fingertips.

"I assume a lady is involved," Chance mused.

Alek chewed and swallowed. "Good assumption," he said, brushing crumbs from his beard as he watched Alessandra walk over to a hand-painted sign announcing a cornfield maze before waving him over.

Her face was bright and alive with her eagerness. It tugged at his heart.

"She must be special, bro," Chance said.

"That she is," Alek admitted, before ending the call and walking over to join her.

Darkness reigned in Passion Grove and the illumination from the black steel lampposts was soft, breaking up the shadows cast by the trees lining the streets. Alek and Alessandra walked the few blocks from the orchard to her estate, and although the town was already relatively safe, she felt secure in his presence. Even the night chill of October wasn't quite as biting with him at her side and his strong arm resting across her shoulders.

"That wasn't so bad, was it?" she asked, breaking the comfortable silence as they walked past the wrought iron fences surrounding properties of sizable homes all set back from the street three hundred feet or more per local ordinance.

Alek shook his head. “No, it wasn’t. I really liked sitting by the campfire after the hayride and listening to the music.”

“Good,” she said.

They fell into that easy silence again, eventually coming to the beginning of the private road leading to her estate. Her all-black golf cart was sitting where they left it that morning. Alessandra removed the key from her back pocket and handed it to Alek before climbing onto the passenger seat. She settled her hand on his thigh as he drove them down the length of the paved road lit with lampposts, as well.

The gate opened as they neared it and they both waved at the security camera as they passed.

“It really is a beautiful house,” Alek said when the view of it came into sight.

“Thank you,” she said.

The white up-lighting gave the expansive mansion a soft glow that illuminated it in the darkness surrounding it. It was grand but still welcoming.

“You wanna check on your fam?” he asked.

“Speed up, please,” she said.

Alek chuckled as he accelerated past the house and under the stone carport. “Sometimes I want to give them all eviction notices in one hand and leases to their own homes in the other,” she said. “I love them but they’re a bit much, you know?”

“Well, I thought that the morning I saw your cousin Victor sneaking into the maid’s quarters,” he said as he pulled to a stop before the guesthouse.

"You what?" she shrieked, looking at him with wide eyes.

Alek looked surprised. "I never told you?" he asked. "Aw, man. It was unreal."

Alessandra turned on the seat of the golf cart to look up at the main house. "I knew he had a side piece across town, but to mess with one of the maids right here under his wife's nose?" she said, her top lip curling in disgust.

Alek leaned over to kiss the corner of her mouth before exiting the cart. "He's bold, that's for sure."

Alessandra was steaming with anger and frustration. "So, I'm paying someone to screw his old horny self?" she said, her tone exasperated. "I ought to go to his suite and pour ice water on his crotch."

Alek picked her up in his arms and kissed her to end her tirade.

She broke the kiss. "Which maid?" she asked as he carried her around the golf cart and into the house.

"Are you going to fire her?" he asked as he reached his foot back to push the door closed before continuing across the living room and down the hall to her master suite.

"Immediately," she spouted.

"Then I don't remember which one," Alek said, setting her on her feet in the bathroom before he removed her coat and began undressing her.

"Alek!"

"I know sometimes we forget because of our privilege, but there is a large segment of people who have to work to provide the basics," he said as he bent to lift each of her feet to remove her boots. "People are one check away from homeless, Alessandra."

"But—"

Alek rose and matched his gaze with hers. "*But* your uncle is in a position of power and it's possible she may feel she cannot tell his old horny self—as you call him—no," he explained.

His tone and manner made her feel like he felt he was talking to an imbecile. "Alek, she works for me, not Victor," she stressed.

"Alessandra, you live in the guesthouse," he exclaimed, as he bent to remove his dark brown ankle boots. "Perhaps she's confused as to just who runs what."

"Or?" she asked, arching a brow.

Alek bit back a smile and shrugged one shoulder as he removed his wool peacoat and tossed it onto the pile of her clothes on the floor. "Or she enjoys screwing the old fart," he said, making a comical face before pulling the light gray sweater and white shirt he wore over his head.

Alessandra eyed the hard definition of Alek's abdomen. "Do you work out?" she asked.

"Of course," he said, unbuttoning his denims and letting them and his boxers drop down his legs before kicking them free with his feet.

"So what do I do? Nothing?" she asked, unbuttoning and removing her snug jeans and panties with much more effort than he had.

Alek walked across the room to turn on the shower; he looked back over his shoulder. "About?" he asked, his face confused.

Alessandra removed her socks and balled them together to throw. It landed solidly against one hard butt cheek. "The horny fart and the maid," she said.

"Oh…um…stay out of it or deal with Victor, because you could fire her and he could just get it going with the new one—young or old, cute or not," he said. "Men talk a lot of ying-yang about a woman's looks but trust me, ugly women get the business, too, especially when the wrong head is making decisions."

Alessandra looked aghast. "That's terrible."

"But very true." He walked down the length of the bathroom with his penis swinging across the top of his thighs before he scooped her up into his arms again and carried her into the shower already filling with steam.

"Alek, but what—"

"No, enough about the horny old fart and the maid," he said, walking them under the spray of the rainfall showerhead as he set her on her feet. "It's time for the horny *young* fart and the billionaire heiress."

After a long day out in the elements, she had to admit that a shower was perfection. She tilted her face, leaning back with a sigh to let the water coat her body. She was startled at the feel something against her belly and opened her eyes to find Alek washing her with a lathered cloth. Her belly. Her back. Shoulders. Arms and then her breasts.

Their eyes locked at that and they shared a soft smile.

With obvious reluctance, he withdrew to rinse and lather the cloth again.

"I've never been bathed before," she whispered into the thick stream before turning to press her hands against the wall and arch her back as she offered him her buttocks.

Alek slapped one smooth brown cheek with the

back of his hand before he massaged the cloth over her intimacy and inner thighs before cleansing her buttocks.

She looked back over her shoulder, her mouth forming a circle as he raised the cloth high in the air to squeeze, sending the warm suds drizzling down her cheeks and the back of her thighs. He grabbed the base of his hard, curving length, propping one foot up on the bench running down the length of the massive shower, to slide his sudsy hardness over the smooth expanse of her cheeks. She raised up on her toes and reached back to push his hand away and ease his hardness inside her.

They both hissed in pleasure as she wiggled her hips back and forth until she was filled with him to the hilt. His hardness divided her. His thickness spread her. His heat infused her. "Yes," she said with a deep, guttural moan that was wild.

Alek bent his legs and began pumping inside her as he dug his fingers into her wet and shiny bottom as the water showered down on them, slickening each stroke. He bit his bottom lip as he looked down at the sight of his thick inches sliding in and out of her, its dark skin shiny from both the water and her juices.

Alessandra bent over to wrap her hands around her ankles.

He cried out as her walls tightened down on his hardness. "Damn, Alessandra!"

She bent her legs wide and arched her back, circling her hips and pulling downward on his hard length until she was able to kiss the smooth tip with the plump lips of her privates before sliding her core up again.

Alek's legs weakened as he shook his head and reached out to the wall for support.

He got harder inside her as she continued that up-and-down slide with a kiss on the tip over and over again.

Alek grabbed her cheeks to stop her as he felt his nut build up in a rush. "No," he begged, stepping back and removing his inches from inside her.

Alessandra stood up, wiping the water and her wet hair from her face as she turned to find him walking down the length of the shower away from her. "What's wrong, Alek?" she asked.

He turned, his hard-on still hard and curving away from his rock-hard body as he pressed his hands to his hips. "I tapped out. I was about to nut. I couldn't take it," he admitted, looking frustrated.

She smiled even as her clit and heart both pulsed with life and desire. Want. Need. She walked to him through the thick steam and pressed his back to the tiled wall. He slid down onto the bench and she straddled his hips, guiding her womanhood onto his hardness as she cupped his face. She smiled and pressed her knees on the wall on either side of his body as she lowered her head to suck his mouth into hers.

Alek moaned, bringing his trembling hands up to cup her breasts and stroke her hard nipples with his thumbs as she began to ride him with a small and tight rotation of her hips.

He felt all of her against him, gripping him and pleasing him. The way she made love to him with such slowness as she sucked gently at his tongue and looked into his eyes touched something deep inside him. There was a shift. His chest felt filled with lightness even as his heart continued to pound with the wildness of a racehorse. He brought one of his hands up to lightly grasp her chin and he slid the other around her body to press to her lower back.

Alessandra had never felt so connected to him before. She broke their kiss to sweetly suck his forehead as he lightly bit her chin, his hand pressing her body closer to him until her soft breasts cushioned his hard chest and the feel of his arm around her body made her feel cherished and protected.

They both gasped and she looked down at him just as he looked up at her. Their mouths gaped as they breathed in each other and the steam in that small space between them. They were connected. Lost in each other. Pleasure personified. Emotions on overload.

"Come with me," she whispered into the steam, leaning back in his embrace with a deep sigh as she worked in snakelike motion that thrust her breasts and hard nipples upward as her tight, wet, hot core eased up and down the length of him with a slowness that caused them both to ache.

Alek was mesmerized by the sight of her as she rode him with ease. He leaned forward to suck at the valley between her breasts as she tilted her head back and called his name.

Together their climax was stoked. Their pleasure was in sync. They knew their release would be so good. Their anticipation was intense.

Both cried out in pleasure as they reached their sizzling pinnacle.

Alek's hold on her supple body tightened as he

coated her walls with spasms of release that left him spent.

Alessandra worked her hips and the muscles of her walls to empty him as tiny explosions of pleasure burst inside her until she was lost to time and place. Nothing mattered but pushing herself over the edge until she felt like she was free-falling through space.

Both were speechless, shaken and moved far more than either wanted to admit.

Lazy Sunday mornings had become their thing, and the next morning was no exception. They didn't awaken until well after noon and even then, they remained in bed, lounging in pajamas or comfortable clothes, watching the Sunday morning news programs, reading the print papers, watching movies or sports, and nibbling off the tray of delicacies usually Alessandra retrieved from the kitchen of the main house.

Sundays were bittersweet because it signaled the end of their retreat and the return to the facade that they weren't deep into the throes of a sexy affair. They protected their weekends in Passion Grove, even agreeing to avoid talking business when they were alone together.

And when the night reigned, they both hated the call from her security requesting permission to admit Alek's driver to pick him up.

Alek would hitch his caramel leather duffel bag high on his shoulder and reach for Alessandra's hand to pull her into a tight embrace as he pressed kisses to her forehead and cheek. She said nothing, afraid that she would plead with him not to go because she wasn't sure that he wouldn't deny her request, so she just accepted his kisses, set aside her regrets and turned her back to keep from watching him walk out the house to climb into the rear of his car.

And she knew it was silly when they would see each other the next day, but there was just something about those weekends in Passion Grove.

*Three days later*

"Can I get you anything, sir?" Huntsman asked.

Alek took a sip of his cognac as his grip tightened on the glass, and he checked his Patek Philippe watch. He and Alessandra were supposed to be having dinner at his penthouse apartment in Tribeca, but she had yet to show and she was more than twenty minutes late. *Where is she?*

"No, I'm fine, Huntsman," he said, reaching in his pocket for iPhone.

He called her as he paced the length of the forty-four-foot great room of his loft-style apartment of nearly six thousand square feet. Her phone rang several times and went to voice mail. He didn't bother to leave a message.

He was beginning to get concerned. Alessandra was punctual to a fault.

Releasing a heavy breath, he strode across the modernly styled room, ignoring the polished bocote wood dining room table set for their dinner, and jogged up the wood and black steel staircase to the second level.

*Bzzz.*

He stopped on his path across the second foyer into the glass-enclosed sunroom to look down at his phone still in his hand. A text from Alessandra. *Thank you, God, she's okay.*

"'In a business dinner with Omar Freed. Have to cancel our plans. Will call as soon as we're done,'" he read, his face steadily becoming incredulous.

*Cancel?*

He frowned. *Have I been stood up?*

For dinner with Omar Freed. His frown deepened.

The politician was canvassing for donations and support for his senate campaign, but when both he and Alessandra met him last week at a fund-raiser it was clear his interest in her was personal. He envisioned her sitting across from the tall, handsome man with a smile in her eyes that he thought only he could give her.

His expression darkened and his entire body felt angry with hurt and disappointment that she had so easily forgotten their plans. Needing air, even if it was frigid, he stepped out of the sunroom and onto the spacious terrace running down the entire length of his apartment. He looked out at the industrial-age architecture, converted warehouses and cobblestoned streets that gave the trendy neighborhood its character and charm. As the cold night air whipped around him, he looked over the low-rise buildings at the waterfront of the Hudson River.

Usually the view gave him peace. It was the reason he'd purchased the apartment, but now the sight offered him no respite at all.

With his supple lips still turned downward, he walked back inside, passing the elevator as he strode across the space and down the stairs. "Huntsman," he called out.

His manservant came down the short hall leading from the eat-in chef's kitchen wiping his hands on a cloth. "Sir," he said, wearing a black apron over his signature black shirt and pants.

"You can serve dinner," he said, taking a seat at the dining room table flanked by a black slate focal fireplace wall that was lit, adding warmth and ambience to the room.

"Alone?" Huntsman asked.

"Yes," he stressed. "Unless a man can no longer have dinner at his table like a civilized human being, Huntsman."

Huntsman removed one of the place settings and used a matte black candle snuffer to put out the lit candles. "When dinner for two was planned?"

Alek stared at him when he saw humor in his eyes. "On second thought I'm not hungry," he said, tossing his black cotton napkin atop the table as he slumped down in the chair.

He wiped his bearded chin with his hand as he looked across the table into the fireplace. His stomach was lit with a flame that even it couldn't match. Jealousy had a way of burning the gut of the man it plagued.

Alek couldn't remember the last time a woman brought out the "green-eyed monster" in him. He could barely think straight.

*I love her. I love Alessandra.*

He swore, sitting up to press his elbows into the wood as he rubbed his hands together before placing them against his face.

This wasn't how things were supposed to go. Love was a complication he never expected, but as he sat there envisioning tossing whatever dinner Omar had ordered at him, Alek knew he had to face the truth. What did he do with his love when Alessandra made it clear that she wanted nothing more than sex?

*Maybe she's moving on to Omar?*

He shook his head. He didn't believe that. That was irrational.

Alessandra cared for him. That he knew. But love? That he didn't believe at all.

She was as driven about her career as he was and had never expressed a desire for love and family—things he always wanted in a wife. Things he was not willing to compromise on.

*What do I do now?*

He had played with fire and now he was getting burned.

*Three days later*

It was her first weekend alone in months.

When she got to Passion Grove last night she had thought Alek was there waiting on her and when that didn't happen, she waited up all night thinking he would make an appearance eventually. It took several glasses of wine to relax herself enough to fall asleep on the sofa while the television watched her.

Somewhere in the middle of the night she had awakened with a start, drool dried on her chin as she looked around at the darkness and it set in that Alek had never arrived. She picked up her iPhone to call him, but decided against it.

She had no right to question him or expect anything from him.

The next morning, she was lounging on her window seat swiping through news articles on her iPad when she spotted a photo of Alek and his date at a charity event from the night before. "What the what," she exclaimed softly, her heart pounding and her gut clenched as she enlarged the picture.

Her eyes missed not one detail.

The smile on his handsome face. His hand on her hip. Her beauty. How good they looked together.

*Is she the reason he didn't come to Passion Grove?*

An image of their bodies coupled in passion flashed and she shook her head as she pressed her eyes closed. She seethed with jealousy at the thought of Alek sharing his body with another woman. She knew she had no right. The rules had been clear. No strings. Just sex.

At the idea of Alek loving another woman, tears filled her eyes and a sadness swelled deep in her soul. She shifted the photo and zoomed in on his face. *He really is handsome.*

Her emotions were all over the place and she felt so confused by it all.

*What's wrong with me?*

She sat the tablet down beside her and pulled her knees to her chest, setting her chin in the groove between them. Memories of the lovemaking in the shower just last weekend stuck uppermost in her mind. The passion and emotion had been on overload. Far more than they should have been for a fling.

*You deserve love, my beautiful niece.*

*Is that what this is?* she wondered as a tear raced down her cheek. *Have I fallen for Alek Ansah?*

*The kind of love your parents had for each other.*

She snorted in derision. It definitely wasn't that.

Her father had adored her mother and even after her death he never remarried or had another committed relationship.

*I want that for you. A lifetime without love—real love—is not easy.*

But it wasn't safe and the idea of loving Alek scared her more than anything.

*Tap-tap.*

Alessandra jumped in surprise at her aunt Leonora standing at the window in a chinchilla fur coat with matching hat. She sat her tablet down and rushed over to open the door. "Aunt Leonora, what are you doing out there?" she asked, grabbing her arm and pulling her inside before she closed the door and blocked the November chill.

"I've been watching you moping in this window seat all morning," she said, removing her coat and hat to reveal she wore hot-pink satin pajamas.

Alessandra glanced at the seat and her eyes fell on the tablet. Pain radiated across her chest.

"No houseguest this weekend?" Aunt Leonora asked lightly.

Alessandra shook her head.

Leonora wrapped her arms around her and Alessandra was grateful to be held tightly.

"It's over," she decided, biting her bottom lip as tears welled in her eyes, because she knew it was time to end her physical relationship with Alek before she set herself up for even bigger heartache.

# *Chapter 10*

*Two weeks later*

As Alessandra rode up in the elevator to LuLu's apartment on the Upper East Side, she pulled her compact from her clutch and checked her makeup. She had called in her glam squad. Shiva had delivered an off-the-shoulder brocade fit-and-flare dress by B Michael. Her hairstylist had pulled her hair back in a sleek ponytail that highlighted her diamond chandelier earrings, and her makeup artists had hopefully camouflaged the darkness and puffiness under her eyes from the tears she cried at night.

For the last two weeks Alek had been traveling overseas, personally checking up on some of their subsidiaries, and outside of business they rarely spoke. She'd put up her guard to protect her heart, but it was still broken. The time had long since passed for her to avoid loving Alek.

The elevator doors opened and she was stepping inside the foyer to LuLu's vibrant and colorful apartment filled with tastefully dressed people there for the surprise birthday party she was throwing Alek. As she handed her topper to the uniformed butler and picked up a flute of champagne from those on the table in the foyer, she wondered if she'd made the right choice to attend.

Alessandra greeted those she knew with a cheerful grin and press of her lips to their cheeks, recognizing ADG executives and board members in the mix. She spotted LuLu across the room and made her way toward her. She was hard to miss in a towering head wrap and flowing bejeweled caftan.

"You came, and look how beautiful you look, Alessandra," LuLu said with a stunning red-lipped smile.

They shared a warm hug.

"I didn't bring a gift," Alessandra said. "What do you get the man who has everything?"

LuLu waved her hand dismissively. "He won't mind. Let me tell you a little something about my sweet eldest son," she said, wrapping her arm around Alessandra's as they moved through the mingling crowd with ease. "Every year on his birthday he buys me a gift to thank me for bringing him into the world."

Alessandra took a sip of her champagne, imagining a showy expensive gift.

LuLu extended her arm. A delicate charm bracelet dangled around her wrist. "It arrived this morning. And every little charm has meaning. It was a very thoughtful gift," she said, stroking it with her fingertips.

*Yes, it is.*

LuLu came to a stop and faced Alessandra. "He appears hard and unreachable, Alessandra, but my son is a good man with a great heart and integrity," she said. "I'll admit he won't show it easily, but once he does he holds nothing back."

Alessandra tried in vain to pull from the tricks of the trade she'd relied on the last five years to present the right image, to be stoic, even cold. In that moment, she failed and knew she had to flee before her tears rose and fell. "You're very lucky, Ms. Ansah, to have such a good son," she said before walking away quickly, pressing her nails into the flesh of her palm to shock herself out of her feelings.

She stopped before a wall of Ghanaian artwork and artifacts that were vibrant against the stark white of the wall. She leaned in to study a picture of a beautiful little girl of about ten who was wet with her hair plastered to her scalp by the water. She didn't know whether to be drawn into figuring out the emotions in her brown eyes or deciding whether it was a digital photo or a painting. *Wow.*

"It's a painting by Ghanaian artist Jeremiah Quarshie."

Alessandra stepped back and smiled at Samira standing beside her looking radiant in a bright red strapless dress that glowed against her chocolate skin. "Hello, Samira," she said. "How have you been?"

Samira smiled at her. "Patiently waiting to hear from you," she said, her eyes twinkling with humor but still determined.

Alessandra flushed with guilt. The Jubilee celebration seemed so long ago. She had gotten so lost in Alek that she hadn't given Samira's request for help any further thought. "I did speak to Alek about it, but I admit I got distracted. Forgive me," she said, reaching out to squeeze the woman's hand.

Samira clasped hers back. "The birthday boy is a handful, right?" she said, nodding in understanding.

Alessandra's heart swelled with sadness. Even with her conflicting feelings on her relationship with Alek, she had missed him during the last two weeks. "Yes, he is."

Samira eyed her oddly.

"What?" Alessandra asked, looking down at herself.

Samira's eyes brightened with awareness before she smiled. "Alek, Alek, Alek," she said. "Good luck, love."

She turned and walked away.

Alessandra didn't stop her or bother to convince her otherwise of whatever she revealed in her face about her feelings for Alek. *I should go.*

LuLu clapped her hands. "Alek is on his way up," she said, motioning for the music playing softly in the background to end as Samira and Naim joined her by the elevator.

Alessandra felt so anxious she was light-headed.

"Where is Chance?" LuLu asked, turning to look about the crowd until she spotted him and waved urgently. "Come on."

Over the rim of her glass Alessandra eyed the tall, handsome man making his way through the crowd in a navy blazer, shirt and slacks. She'd never met Chance Castillo but she knew he was Alek's best friend. He reached LuLu and her children just a moment before the elevator doors opened.

Alek's eyes widened as he stood there in all black.

"Surprise!"

Alek playfully stepped back onto the elevator, but Naim and Chance rushed behind him to pull him into the foyer before they each hugged him close and patted his back.

Alessandra felt left out as she stood there in the background watching his family and friends greet him. For months, they had created a world with no one but them. Being there in the crowd felt so achingly different from the intimate moments they shared.

When Alek began to look about the crowd she wondered for whom he was searching, until his eyes landed on hers. They locked. She couldn't hold back her smile when his face lit at the sight of her. As he made his way through the crowd, she was unable to resist doing the same. In that moment, she was willing to risk it all just to feel his lips on hers. Be damned who saw.

Alessandra's steps faltered before she came to a stop at the sight of a beautiful woman in a crimson-red strapless jumpsuit stepping in front of Alek, pressing her hands to the lapels of his blazer before she eased them up around his neck.

He lightly grabbed her wrists and lowered her arms to keep her from wrapping them around his neck as he cast Alessandra an apologetic look. She was thankful no one was aware of the little drama that just unfolded as she gave him a tight smile and raised her flute to him in a toast before she turned and walked away.

*I knew I shouldn't have come.*

Stiffening her back, she moved away from the crowd. "Restroom, please?" she asked a passing waiter.

"Last door at the end of this hall," he directed her.

Alessandra nodded and hurried down the hall, quickly entering and closing the door behind herself. She licked her lips and sat her flute on the marble counter as she studied her reflection. Her regret was palpable.

*I never should have started this with Alek.*

*I never should have let him in my heart.*

*I never should have come here.*

She swore in a harsh whisper, closing her eyes and tilting her head back as she fought so hard to maintain her composure.

She opened her eyes and was startled to see the woman in the red jumpsuit in the reflection behind her. *What the...*

"So, you're Alessandra," she said.

Alessandra turned, her eyes shifting to the door she forgot to lock and back to the woman. "And you are?" she asked.

"I'm Kenzay Ansah, Alek's wife."

"Ex-wife," Alessandra countered, feeling the woman's animosity radiate toward her. "And?"

*Am I going to have to hurt her?*

Kenzay smiled before she shifted her eyes past Alessandra to study her reflection and play with her hair. "*And...* I wanted to meet the little sucker Alek was so desperate to get rid of that he was willing to seduce her into submission...if his attempts to sway the board to vote you out failed," she taunted, locking her cold eyes on her again.

For a moment, Alessandra felt taken back to her time as Alex, the girl who was afraid of her own shadow, lacked confidence and just wanted to be forgotten.

But just for a moment.

That wasn't her any longer.

"Kenzay, I don't know you and you don't know me, but if you think coming in here brimming with insecurity and immaturity, hoping that I will dwell with you there, is a good look then you are not only desperate and attention-seeking but dead-ass wrong," she said, her voice stone-cold and her eyes brimming with her disdain. "Let me introduce you, little girl, to what you hope to be one day, which is a grown-ass woman. Go find someone else to play with."

Alessandra picked up her flute of champagne and her clutch before leaving the woman standing there with her mouth open in shock.

*Where did she go? Where is Alessandra?*

After he bypassed Kenzay, Alessandra turned away from him. He followed behind her but the party guests kept stopping him to wish him well and he lost sight of her.

Although he knew nothing of the party and hadn't invited his ex-wife, he felt an urgency to explain himself to Alessandra. Things were already so off between them.

He never reminded her that she'd stood him up but quietly clung to his anger and jealousy, pulling a deliberate stunt by taking another woman to an event he initially had no plans on attending to avoid going to Passion Grove. It was an irrational move and childish act that he regretted.

And so he fled under the premise of work out of the country, needing space to grapple with his feelings for her—his want of her.

Over the last couple of weeks, Alek had also noticed a shift in Alessandra. The warmth in her voice disappeared and their conversations outside of business were brief. He wondered if their time together was over. He hoped not.

He missed her.

He loved her.

And he decided that he loved her enough to lay it all on the line and risk disappointment and hurt so that he would never wonder "what if."

When he entered his mother's apartment he was surprised by the birthday party, but not pleased. His intention had been to spend a little time with his family, collect his gift, blow out candles and then head out to find Alessandra. His anxiousness about working the room for a little while before taking his leave evaporated when he spotted Alessandra standing out among the crowd with her eyes locked on him.

Nothing had mattered to him more than getting to her.

And then Kenzay swooped in.

*Did she leave?*

He turned and spotted her just as she came out of the guest bathroom. "Alessandra," he called out, heading toward her.

She met him halfway, surprising him when she grabbed his wrist and pulled him out onto the balcony.

"I missed you," he moaned, reaching for her hips and leaning in to finally kiss her.

Alessandra tilted her head back from him and scowled.

*Uh-oh.*

"Did you try to rally the board to vote me out?"

she asked, crossing her arms over her chest as she eyed him.

*Damn.*

Any ideas of sharing a passionate kiss with her quickly faded. He released a heavy breath and looked up to the dark skies.

"Wow, Alek," she said in disbelief. "Just…wow."

He looked at her. "That was in the beginning, Alessandra. That was before we even linked up to—"

"Screw?" she interjected angrily.

He frowned. "Don't do that, Alessandra. I was going to say before we linked up on the airline deal."

"Don't do that?" she asked with calm. "What you shouldn't have done, Alek Ansah, is seduce me just to weaken my interest in the business and then let your ex-wife—and God knows who else—know all about it."

Alek's face immediately filled with guilt. "That was a joke, Alessandra, I swear," he said, remembering the dinner party at Chance's apartment.

He reached for her, and she shook her head and held up her hand as she stepped back. His heart ached to see the tears brimming in her eyes as she fought so hard to maintain her calm.

"You'll do anything to get me out of the company," she said with a bitter laugh. "Just like you threatened to cut your sister off to keep her from entering the business. Right?"

Alek felt desperate, as if he were trying to contain sand that slipped through his open fingers.

"I love you, Alessandra," he said, praying she could see the sincerity in his eyes.

"No, you do not," she said plainly. "Don't go that far, Alek. Don't cross every line."

"I love you," he stressed, grasping her arm and trying to lock eyes with her. "Please believe me."

"Stay the hell away from me if it has nothing to do with ADG," she said, roughly jerking her arm from his grasp and entering the apartment through the balcony door before disappearing into the crowd.

"Damn," Alek swore, trying to follow behind her, but he was surrounded by his guests.

He lost sight of her and knew he couldn't catch up to her.

Curiosity was killing LuLu.

She eased away from the party, entered her master suite and crossed the room to step out onto the balcony. She shivered in the coldness but she still clutched the metal railing of her balcony and looked down at the row of chauffeured cars on the street below. It wasn't hard to spot Alessandra's vintage Jaguar, nor for her to pick out her driver among those chauffeurs braving the night chill to pass their time waiting together.

"Roje," she whispered, pressing a hand to her pounding heart.

"What you shouldn't have done, Alek Ansah, is seduce me just to weaken my interest in the business and then let your ex-wife—and God knows who else—know all about it."

First LuLu's eyes widened and then her mouth dropped at the sound of Alessandra's raised voice. They had to be on the balcony in the great room. *Alek did what?*

"That was a joke, Alessandra, I swear."

*Oh, Alek.*

LuLu was torn between rudeness at eavesdropping and a mother's innate curiosity about her children's lives. And she did listen on and she felt like weeping because it was clear they both were hurting.

"I love you. Please believe me."

LuLu heard the raw emotion in her son's voice and knew him well enough to know he spoke the truth of his heart. *Alek is in love.*

"Stay the hell away from me if it has nothing to do with ADG."

And Alessandra loved him, as well. That level of hurt and anger were the shadows to being deeply in love. That LuLu knew as she took off across her bedroom suite in her heels. She denied herself happiness and love. She did not want that for any of her children.

*They already sneaked this past me.*

LuLu made it down the hall and onto the elevator behind Alessandra just before the doors closed. She looked down to make sure her flowing caftan hadn't been caught. "Come, come, come, come, come," LuLu said, beckoning her with her fingers at seeing the young woman's emotions on overload.

They shared a brief look before LuLu closed the distance and embraced her. Moments later, Alessandra's body shook with her tears. "I know about you and Alek," she admitted as she stroked the woman's back and gently rocked their bodies. "I overheard your argument on the balcony."

"Oh no," Alessandra wailed. "Did everyone hear us?"

"No, just me," LuLu said, leaning back to look at

her as she wiped away the track of her tears with her thumb.

The elevator came to a stop and LuLu took Alessandra's hand in hers to lead her to a sitting area in the lobby. "I know you think I am saying this because he is my son, but I heard the love he has for you in my son's voice, Alessandra," she said. "Before I was his mother, I was a woman who lived and loved and lost."

Alessandra removed tissues from her clutch and pressed them to her cheeks. "I'm sorry but I don't believe that," she admitted.

"What do you believe?" LuLu asked.

"I believe that Alek betrayed me. I believe he would go to any lengths to oust me from the company," Alessandra said, releasing a heavy breath before she continued. "I believe I am so disappointed that I feel betrayed by my own heart."

LuLu's ached for her. "The only advice I have is to remember the time you shared and follow your gut if you really believe all of it was fake. I believe you're smarter than that, Alessandra. Don't you?"

"I thought I was smart enough not to risk everything I worked so hard to establish in business for a man, and well, I guess I wasn't that smart, after all," she said, rising to her feet. "I left my jacket."

"Would you like me to go up and get it?" LuLu asked.

"No, that's okay," she said, taking out her phone. "I'll just make sure my driver turns up the heat."

LuLu looked up at her. "Your parents loved each other and in time they were lost to each other, but I promise you neither one regretted the love. They would want that for you. I want that for my son."

Alessandra's lingering sadness was clear. "Thank you for your kindness," she said.

LuLu rose as well, walking her to the door.

The doorman held the door open for them.

"Thank you, William," LuLu told him before turning back to Alessandra. "I hope you think of what I've said."

Alessandra remained quiet.

Roje spotted them and came walking up to them, quietly standing beside Alessandra with his eyes resting on LuLu.

"Life is too short to deny yourself love," LuLu said, unable to look away from him.

Alessandra hugged her. "Seems like advice you could use as well, Ms. Ansah," she said before turning and walking away.

LuLu barely felt the cold as she stood there lost in the regret in Roje's eyes.

"Ms. Ansah." Roje greeted her with a nod before finally breaking their stare and following behind Alessandra.

She watched as he helped Alessandra into the rear of the Jaguar before looking back at her. With one last glance at him, she walked back inside determined to be okay with her decision to deny herself love.

Alek was on the chase.

He wasn't a violent man. He didn't want to lay hands on his ex-wife, but he would pay good money to lay eyes on hers.

He wiped his mouth with his hands as he flipped over his iPhone and called Kenzay's phone number for the third time. It went straight to voice mail. "Shit," he swore.

Alek looked up as Chance and his fiancée, Helena, came toward him where he stood away from the crowd by the entrance to the kitchen.

"You're missing the party," Chance said, handing Alek the extra glass of champagne he carried.

"Have either of you seen Kenzay?" he asked them.

Chance shook his head.

"She left," Helena said, the diamonds of her numerous bracelets and her engagement ring shining brightly as she tucked her blond hair behind her ear. "Something about a headache."

Alek gritted his teeth as he slid his phone into the inside pocket of his blazer. "She's the damn headache," he muttered.

Helena made a face. "That's not nice, Alek," she said before playfully pouting.

Chance and Alek shared a brief look.

"What isn't nice is her telling Alessandra that I was planning a hostile takeover of the business and—"

"Weren't you, though?" Helena said lightly with a wince.

Alek looked at Chance again.

"And that I planned to seduce her to get her to leave the business," he added, his ire rising.

Helena seemed oblivious to it. "You *did* say it. I was there," she said.

Alek frowned. "So, your moral compass says it's okay to be mean and spiteful to a woman you don't even know just because you're jealous?" he asked, his tone hostile. "Then what does that say about you?"

Chance eased in between them. “We’re gonna head on out, Alek,” he said.

Alek held up his hands. Helena irked his spirit but she still was his best friend’s bride-to-be. “Nope. Y’all stay. I’m leaving,” he said, turning and striding away.

He reached the foyer, happy that the partygoers didn’t even notice him as he summoned the elevator. The doors opened and he was surprised to see his mother exiting. He noticed her sadness. “Ma, you okay?” he asked.

She forced a smile that didn’t reach her eyes. “I wasn’t happy to overhear that my son even joked about playing with a woman’s heart for any reason,” she said.

His broad shoulders slumped and he looked down at his feet. “It’s all a misunderstanding,” he explained.

She grasped his chin and tilted his head up. “Then go fix it,” she said before patting his cheek and then gently nudging him onto the elevator. “We’ll cut the cake and open presents tomorrow. Okay?”

“I will, but first it’s time to get some clarity with Kenzay,” he said.

“Make it clear that when she invites herself to a party she shouldn’t upset invited guests, so she is no longer welcome in my home,” LuLu said with a broad smile just before the elevator doors closed.

Alek couldn’t get the look of hurt and betrayal in Alessandra’s eyes out of his mind. He hurt because he knew she was hurt.

*You’ll do anything to get me out of the company.*

There was a time he would have, but she had gained his respect.

The elevator doors opened and he quickly strode across the marble lobby out the door to the street. Before he reached the curb, Julius was pulling the black Bentley Mulsanne out of his parking spot down the street and easing to a stop in front of the building. "The Peninsula Hotel, Julius," he said as he soon as he slid onto the rear seat and closed the door.

The Peninsula was Kenzay's go-to spot when she was in town.

As Julius sped up the street, Alek thought he spotted a flash of red as they passed a parked SUV. "Pull over, Julius," he said, already reaching for the handle before the car came to a complete stop.

Alek jogged up the street and pulled open the door to the SUV. Kenzay looked at him before glancing away with a bored sigh.

"Hey," the driver yelled out, turning around in his seat.

"What was your purpose tonight, Kenzay?" he asked, his voice cold and unrelenting.

"Awww, did Kenzay make someone cry?" she asked, her voice petulant as she pulled a compact from her clutch. It lit her face when she opened it, exposing her smugness.

Alek paused as he looked at her and really saw her for the first time. "What did Alessandra ever do to you?" he asked.

She snapped her compact closed as looked at him. "She took your attention off of me," she said. "No other woman has ever made you reject me, *and* in public. That was a first for us, and if you ever want to have me again it best be the last."

This was about her ego and her belief that she controlled him.

"I love her, Kenzay," he said. "If I lose Alessandra because of you—"

"Because of *me*?" Kenzay retorted. "I shouldn't have that much power in your silly little relationship. If I'm able to make it crumble just like that…then it was already broken somewhere."

He hated that there was truth in her words. His relationship with Alessandra—if it could be called that—had not been perfect at all. The hesitance to be together. The secrecy of their dealings. The resistance to accepting her just as easily in the boardroom as the bedroom.

"We're done, Kenzay," he said, his anger with her dissipating. "It's time we both moved on for good."

She looked at him for a long time. Even the driver shifted uncomfortably in his seat. "She gets the love you never gave me?" she asked.

He shook his head. "I'm calling foul on that, Kenzay. Alessandra has nothing to do with the love we didn't have for each other," he stressed, stepping back and reaching for the door.

"You'll call me, but will I answer, that's the question," she said, her feigned hurt gone and replaced by her conceit again.

"Goodbye, Kenzay," Alek said, closing the car door firmly before he turned and walked away.

He didn't flinch or look back when Kenzay began screaming expletives out the window of the SUV detailing just what he could with both his head and his goodbyes. He was thankful when he climbed back in the Bentley and closed the door, shutting her tirade off as he called Alessandra's phone.

It rang just once.

She was sending his calls to voice mail.

He slumped down in the back of the car and covered his eyes with his fingers. He felt sick.

"Where to now?" Julius asked.

"Passion Grove," he said, sitting up to text Alessandra.

I LOVE YOU, ALESSANDRA. WE NEED TO TALK. PLEASE ANSWER. PLEASE CALL ME.

He had no shame. He wanted her back.

During the nearly one-hour drive Alek forced himself not to continue to text her like an obsessed stalker.

As they drove through the quiet streets of Passion Grove he thought back to all the time they shared there. An ache of loss radiated across his chest.

Julius pulled the car up to the gate of her estate and Alek jumped out of the car to walk up to the security video camera. "Hey, fellas," he said with a wave. "Is Alessandra home?"

"Good evening, Mr. Ansah," a voice said through the intercom. "I'm sorry, but Ms. Dalmount has alerted us not to allow you on the estate, sir."

He turned just as Julius respectfully rolled the driver's-side window up.

"Could you call her, please?" he asked.

"We've been instructed not to, sir."

Through the gate, Alek looked up the long drive as he paced. The irony of it all was not lost on him. He finally laid his feelings out for her and he could understand her inability to trust that the words were true.

He moved back over to the security camera. "Were

you instructed not to call anyone else on the property?" he asked, thinking quickly on his feet.

The pause was lengthy.

"No, sir," the male voice finally answered.

"Then please call her aunt Leonora for me," he said.

As he waited, Alek knew the sense of urgency he felt was brought on by his guilt. He had tried to orchestrate her removal from ADG and for that he had been wrong.

He turned as light suddenly radiated across his body. It gradually brightened. Soon he distinguished the golf cart coming down the drive. He slid his hands into his pockets as he stood facing the gate. It came to a stop and he watched as Leonora exited wearing a fur with a hood. She came to stand on the other side of the gate as she lit a cigarette.

"Hello, Alek," she said, the tip of her extra-long cigarette reddening as she inhaled. "The camera and intercoms are off."

He nodded as he stepped closer to the gate. "I need to speak with Alessandra," he said.

"Listen, I can see a lot from my bedroom balcony. I honestly don't think you spent every weekend for the last three months cooped up in that guesthouse with my niece just to get her away from ADG," she said firmly. "The vote could have done that. Okay?"

"Okay," he said, surprised that she knew of their relationship.

"She's gone, Alek," she said, pausing to take another draw. "Best advice I can give you is to allow her the time she needs. Okay?"

He felt gut-punched as he nodded and stepped back from the gate. She was gone. He remembered when he wanted that so badly. Now it broke his heart. With a final nod of understanding he walked back to the Bentley and got in the rear. As Julius reversed, the lights from the golf cart and the red flame of her cigarette eventually disappeared.

# *Chapter 11*

*One month later*

Alessandra smiled as Roje drove her past the large bronze sign welcoming them back to Passion Grove, New Jersey. Snow covered the tops of buildings and the ground. Christmas decor was in abundance. It was the holiday season.

"Feel good to be back?" Roje asked, eyeing her in the rearview mirror.

"Yes," she admitted without hesitation.

"I'm very happy you're back," he said. "Driving Marisa around has been an…adventure."

Alessandra nodded, glancing out the window at the line of storefronts before glancing back at him. "Thank you for letting me know what's going on with her, Roje," she said. "I'm disappointed to hear her partying has advanced to drug use."

"She needs you," was all that he said.

Alessandra had been working out of the London offices for the last month, needing a break from Alek and her foolish feelings for him. That night she had fled home to Passion Grove, falling into a crying heap at her aunt's feet in her bedroom suite. When Alek came to the security gate she had been safely ensconced in a ball in the middle of her aunt's bed and Leonora had gone down to the gate to lie to him for her. Alessandra had never appreciated her more.

The next morning, she packed an overnight bag and headed out on the company jet for an early flight to London. There was an executive penthouse apartment in London, but Alek had resided there for five years and she knew it would be too much to take. She spent one night at the Four Seasons Hotel and the next day moved into a spacious four-bedroom, four-bathroom furnished home after a call to Harrods Estates. Shiva arrived for the day to shop for her wardrobe, organize her massive walk-in closet, and find a hairdresser/makeup artist to use while she was in London.

That Monday she was spit-shined and polished for her first day working out of the London office without a bit of notice to her team of her arrival. That had been fun to see them all scramble to accommodate one of their bosses.

Between exploring England and work, she had almost been able to forget him.

Almost.

Her hurt was still there. It still nagged at her, but time had dulled it to an ache and not a piercing pain that radiated. She felt better prepared to return to the offices Monday with her head held high and her dignity and poise intact.

As they drove past the frozen heart-shaped pond, she sat up to look at all the townspeople either ice-skating or figure skating, their faces filled with joy and happiness. *I'm home*, she thought, sitting back when the frivolity on the lake was no longer in sight.

Soon they were coasting up the long driveway to the house. "The main house, Roje," she said.

"Luggage, too?" he asked.

"Yes."

He nodded as he pulled to a stop before exiting to open her door and assist her out.

"Thank you, Roje," she said, giving his hand a gentle squeeze before releasing it.

As she walked up the steps she paused, turning to look at Roje removing her hard-side suitcase from the trunk. "Roje, how are you?" she asked.

Myriad emotions showed on his face ranging from surprise to understanding.

He knew she was asking of LuLu Ansah.

He smiled. "The same," he said.

She offered him a smile and left it at that. There was a line of privacy she was trying not to cross. She took it to the line and leaned against it, but she did not want to step over.

As soon as she opened one of the towering double doors to enter the foyer, the twins came running across her path with high-pitched squeals. "Harper and Parker!" she shouted.

They stopped and turned to look at her. Their eyes were wide and their little barrel chests heaved with their exertion.

"Walk where you're going," she said sternly. "You're *not* outside. Respect my house."

They looked at each other briefly before looking back at her.

"Do you understand me?" she asked, knowing they were confused by being disciplined by her. "Yes, ma'am or no, ma'am?"

"Yes, ma'am," they said in unison desolately.

"Shoo-shoo," she said.

They walked away holding hands but soon she heard their feet pounding the floors as they upped it back to a run. Memories of her time in the guest-house with Alek made it uninhabitable for Alessandra and she was moving back into the master suite in the main house. The twins would have to be reined in. In fact, everyone would. Aunt Leonora's drinking. Aunt Brunela's resentment for not being given the same opportunity as her niece. Victor's philandering with staff. His wife's lackluster discipline of the twins.

She walked to the side of the grand staircase to take the hall leading into the dining room. Aunt Leonora stood beside her aunt Brunela, who sat at the table with her head bent and her shoulders shaking with tears.

"I'm sure Marisa is okay, sis," Leonora said, picking up a half-filled glass tumbler of heavily diluted orange.

"Where is Marisa?" Alessandra asked, coming to stand behind one of the parson chairs.

They both looked to her in surprise before coming over to hug her and press a kiss to her cheek.

"Thank God you're back," Brunela said, wiping her tears with a satin handkerchief that was already damp from her weeping. "You're the only one Marisa listens to, Alessandra."

"What happened?" she asked, feeling alarmed.

"She's been partying pretty hard lately," Leonora said. "And didn't come home last night at all."

Brunela cried out in anguish and slumped back down onto her chair.

*Driving Marisa around has been an...adventure.*

Roje.

She turned and quickly strode down the length of the hall.

"Alessandra, where are you going?" Leonora called behind her.

"Hopefully to find Marisa," Alessandra said over her shoulder before she flung the door open and raced down the steps.

Roje was just pulling off in the Jag.

Alessandra waved frantically to get his attention.

He stopped and lowered the window.

"Did you drive Marisa last night?" she asked as she rushed over to the car.

He shook his smooth bald head. "She drove one of the cars to a weekend party."

"You know where?" Alessandra asked, already climbing in the back of the car.

"She texted me the address when she wanted me to drive her at first."

"Take me there, please," she said, rotating her head on her neck to remove the tension steadily building.

"Right away," Roje said, accelerating down the drive.

As he drove through the streets of Passion Grove and then out toward Manhattan, Alessandra wrestled with whether to share with her aunts what Roje told her about Marisa using cocaine. She'd come home from London earlier than she planned to try to get her cousin in rehab.

Roje slowed the Jaguar to a stop in front of a modest brick home in a suburban neighborhood forty minutes outside of Midtown Manhattan. Alessandra looked around at the tree-lined streets filled with modest homes with cars and SUVs parked nearly bumper-to-bumper. "You sure this is the right address, Roje?" she asked.

His head bent as he looked down at his phone to double-check the address. "This is it," he said, looking through the driver's-side window.

"Okay, I don't see any parking, so you circle the block and come back to pick us up," she said, climbing from the back of the car and pulling the red wool coat she wore tighter around the white T-shirt and distressed jeans she wore with high-heeled boots.

Alessandra walked up the snow-covered path to the small stoop. She was admittedly nervous as she rang the doorbell. She looked up and down the stretch of homes as she waited.

The door opened and a tall, slender woman with bright red hair and freckles stood there. "Yes?" she said.

"I was looking for Marisa. Is she still here?" Alessandra said, looking past her at the living room. Her eyes widened to see her cousin stark naked and dancing atop a table.

She brushed past the redhead, already removing her coat, as she reached up to snatch Marisa down off the table. The crowd of people in the living room either laughed or complained. Alessandra ignored them all as she wrapped the coat around her cousin's nakedness.

"We're leaving now," she said as Marisa tried to resist her, but was too high to muster the strength to succeed.

*Boom.*

Alessandra froze as the front door flew wide open and the police in SWAT gear rushed inside the house as people scattered.

"Everybody down," several police officers roared.

"Uh-oh, we in trouble now, coz," Marisa whispered, before bursting into a fit of foolish giggles.

More than thirty days had passed and his love for Alessandra had not faded one bit. But she also had not returned from London or spoken to him outside of conference calls to deal with their business. He ached for her. Still.

With a sigh, he looked down at a photo he'd taken of her the night of the Jubilee Ball from across the room. He'd never told her about the picture, and over the last month he'd often turn to it when he missed her in his life, his bedroom and their boardroom. She wasn't at all the wife he envisioned over the years but he couldn't imagine loving anyone else the way he cared for Alessandra.

He put away his phone and looked over his shoulder from where he sat at the front of the church's sanctuary. Although Chance and Helena had planned their wedding in just a month, the church was filled with their guests and elaborately decorated with flowers and white satin. Through the clear glass panes at the top of the entry doors he spotted Chance and Helena in the vestibule talking emphatically. She was in her gown and veil, but it was clear Chance's face was lined with anger.

*This ain't looking good.*

When the wedding planner, Olivia Joy, quietly entered the sanctuary Alek rose and made his way to her.

He forced himself to keep his pace slow and leisurely as he made his way down the side aisle, ignoring the curious looks of his own family. "What's going on?" he asked Olivia when he reached her.

She leaned in close. "The wedding's off," she whispered to him.

Alek's eyes widened in surprise. "Okay, let me check on my boy," he said, opening the door when she eased from in front of it.

The front doors to the church were wide open and Chance stood in the doorway taking the brunt of the December chill that blew in. "You okay, Chance?" he asked, coming to stand beside him.

Chance shrugged one shoulder as he shook his head. *"Elegir una esposa más bien por su oído que su ojo,"* he said.

*Choose a wife rather by your ear than your eye.* Alek remained quiet; he didn't know Helena very well and their relationship had been a whirlwind.

"She's gone. She was double-dipping with her ex and seems he didn't have a problem sharing the goodies as long as she wasn't a wife," he said, his voice cold.

Alek winced. He hadn't seen that coming.

"I'm sorry, Chance," he said, reaching over to give his shoulder a solid but comforting pat.

Chance clenched his jaw. *"Usted debe cumplir la aspereza con la aspereza,"* he said, the usual warmth in his eyes replaced with bristling anger.

*You must meet roughness with roughness.*

Alek dropped his hand, surprised by his friend's rage. In all the years of their friendship Chance was the lighthearted, fun-loving one. He rarely turned to fury. "Hey, you all right, man?" he asked.

Chance smiled but it didn't reach his eyes. "Let's go announce the wedding is off and turn the reception into a party, amigo," he said, turning to walk back into the church.

Olivia gave Alek a confused look as Chance strode past her and up the middle of the aisle.

"Take your team to the reception site and remove as much wedding stuff as you can and have the wedding cake completely sliced and put on plates," he said.

She unclipped a walkie-talkie from the waist of her skirt before she walked away.

As Chance spoke briefly with the minister at the front of the church, Alek turned and pulled his phone from the inner pocket of his tuxedo as it vibrated. "Google alert," he said. He had alert sets up for any mention of the Ansah Dalmount Group.

"'Billionaire heiress and ADG co-CEO Alessandra Dalmount arrested in drug bust,'" he read. "Wait. What?"

He read the headline again before opening the article and reading it in its entirety, his eyes widening and his heart pounding furiously. He was lost. *I thought Alessandra was still in London.*

*In jail?*

*A drug bust?*

*This has to be a mistake, right?*

*What the hell?*

The cold felt good.

Alessandra inhaled deeply of it, letting it fill her

lungs and invigorate her. Even one night of captivity had been too much, and freedom was sweet. Not enough to curb the anger that stewed overnight as she sat in a cell but enough where she didn't feel encaged.

"Alessandra—"

Sharply, she put up her hand to silence her cousin as they stood on the sidewalk outside the police station.

"You have a choice to make, Marisa," she said, staring down the street at the bustling traffic, unable to even look at her cousin. She did a double take when she thought she spotted Alek's Bugatti pulling out a parking spot down. She blinked and scrunched her face.

"About what?" Marisa asked.

Alessandra looked down at her, still dressed in her coat with her face puffy and reddish from her overindulgence. "What?" she asked, glancing back down the street.

"You said I have a choice," Marisa said, using the sides of her hands to wipe her eyes.

Putting aside what she considered daydreams, Alessandra nodded as Roje pulled up in the Jaguar and climbed out to hand her a faux fur that was still luxuriously warm. "You okay?" he asked.

"No," she admitted before turning back to her charge. "Rehab or I'm done with you. I will love you always, but you are not coming back into my life or my home as an addict."

"Rehab!" Marisa shrieked, pushing back her wild array of curls that the wind blew in her face.

Alessandra glanced back at her personal attorney, Ngozi Johns, quietly standing off to the side in a brilliant red pantsuit and matching wool coat. "Ms. Johns's staff has located a long-term facility for you to get better mentally and physically, Marisa," she said, pointing to an SUV that double-parked behind the Jaguar. "Rehab with Ms. Johns or back to the estate with me to pack your things and leave."

Marisa's eyes hardened and her mouth became a straight line before she walked down the steps toward the waiting SUV.

"I will call you when we arrive," Ngozi said.

"Thank you very much. I appreciate it—"

Marisa stopped in the middle of the street, causing those passing by to quickly shift to avoid her. "You can't just put me out. I have rights. You have to evict me. Right? Doesn't she have to evict me?" Marisa cried out, her desperation so abundantly clear.

"She's right," Ngozi said, her voice just for Alessandra's ears.

Alessandra came down the steps, brushing off Roje's hand when he reached for her wrist. "Is that how you want to do this? In this moment where you can choose victory or defeat over your own damn life, is that the level you want to sink to? Court? Eviction!" she snapped, her eyes burning with hurt and anger. "Why is it every *damn* time I try to help you, *you* make me suffer for it, Marisa? Huh? Why is that? *Why?*"

Marisa lowered her head.

"Do you understand my career and everything I worked hard for may be over? I have an arrest record. My *mug shot* is *all* over the news," Alessandra stressed, pressing her hand to her chest as she eyed her cousin. "But I didn't think of any of that because I just wanted to help you. And that's how you want this to go down? Because it can. Because I will. So you let me know how we are doing this, Marisa."

"I'm sorry," she mouthed, a single tear racing down her cheek, before she turned and walked to the SUV and climbed inside without looking back.

Alessandra's shoulders dropped as she tucked her hands inside the deep pockets of her coat.

"The board wants to meet with you," Ngozi said, coming to stand beside her.

Alessandra felt like a vise grip closed down on her gut. She'd assumed they'd at least wait until Monday to call her on the carpet. She thought of Alek, something she rarely allowed herself to do, and she couldn't help but envision him with a smug expression as she was voted out of the company. *Just the way he always wanted.*

"Okay," Alessandra said, following Roje to the Jag to climb in the back as he held the door open.

She gave Ngozi a wave before she strode to the SUV and climbed into the rear beside Marisa.

"ADG, Roje," she said, crossing her legs in her distressed jeans as she sank down in the seat and closed her eyes.

As they made the drive to Manhattan, she felt her driver's eyes on her occasionally but she was thankful he respected her need for silence. She felt so embarrassed by having her life—her privacy—wrecked by the arrest. *And now I have to see Alek.*

A dull ache began to radiate across her nape, and by the time they reached the office and she made her way inside via her private entrance, it had not lessened. She entered the bathroom in her office and was thankful to remove every stitch of clothing she was sure still reeked of jail. As she showered and brushed her teeth, tears threatened to fall, but she refused to let them.

Dressed in a long-sleeved black lace dress with a wide skirt and her hair up in a tousled topknot, she felt more like herself as she paced her office waiting the five minutes before the meeting was to begin. She knew the procedure; the meeting had already begun. Decisions were being made. Votes cast. By the time she arrived her fate would be sealed.

Alek would have won.

*Little sucker. Little sucker. Little sucker.*

Alessandra covered her face with her hands, hating how foolish she felt. Still.

*I love you, Alessandra. Please believe me.*

She shook his deceiving words from her thoughts and checked her watch as she sat down, then quickly rose to her feet, leaving her iPhone on the sofa. She smoothed her hair up, straightened the skirt of her dress and stiffened her spine as she walked out of her office and made her way to the boardroom. Pretending she wasn't nervous. Pretending she wasn't embarrassed. Pretending she wasn't still heartbroken.

Her steps faltered at the sight of Ms. Kingsley sitting at the receptionist desk to the right. *Why is she here on a Saturday?*

"Good morning," Alessandra said, giving her a smile.

More pretending.

Ms. Kingsley stood up, her face showing her unease. "Good morning, Ms. Dalmount. The board requested to be alerted when you arrived," she said, her face apologetic.

Alessandra arched a brow. "I think the board is confused as to who owns forty-nine percent of this building, and that's a fact no one can change, Ms.

Kingsley," she said, turning to open both doors to the boardroom at once.

Their vote could affect her position as CEO but not her ownership, and she refused to be disrespected regardless of anything.

All conversation ceased at the sight of her. Several of them looked at each other and shifted uncomfortably in their seats.

Her eyes fell on Alek. A kaleidoscope of emotions washed over her, mostly surprise that he had lost weight and wasn't quite as sharply groomed as usual. They shared a brief look before he focused his gaze out the window.

She took that for guilt and she hated that Alek Ansah could still hurt her.

*Keep it together.*

"Have a seat, Alessandra," Aldrich said, looking out of place in a polo shirt and sweatpants.

She crossed her hands in front of her and eyed each and every board member who would even look at her. "I prefer to stand," she said.

Aldrich shook his head as he patted his hand atop the table. "It's not like that," he said.

"Isn't it, though?" Alessandra returned.

Aldrich sighed. "As you know, an emergency board meeting was called in light of your arrest yesterday," he began. He then met her eyes, the bright blue of his unflinching. "It was an embarrassment to this company and the reputation both Kwame and Frances worked so hard to establish. As the CEO, it could immediately and detrimentally affect our standing, and certainly makes everyone including many in this room question your ability to effectively lead."

She briefly glanced at Alek's stoic profile. "I am not, nor have I ever been on drugs—"

Aldrich held up his hand. "That's good to hear, but it doesn't change the perception that you are," he said. "This was reckless and irresponsible, Alessandra, and made us wonder if you are truly fit to help run this company."

She knew he was right.

At the clearing of a throat, she looked toward Charlie Memminger, one of the few board members who had openly challenged Alessandra consistently.

"There is a little-known market out clause that was put in place by the original underwriters of ADG's initial public offering," he said, picking up a pair of spectacles from the table to slide on as he looked down at the piece of paper. "The clause—basically a morality clause—leaves the opportunity for one or both of the CEOs to be ousted if they do anything to the detriment of the company."

Alessandra was well aware of the clause but remained quiet. She knew with a majority vote by the board of the directors she would keep her stake in the company but be removed from her position and her seat on the board of directors. The arrest was scandalous and handed them a golden ticket to get rid of her.

She held up her hand. "I want a moment to speak because it is my character and my ability to lead that is in question, but it is in fact my leadership and my character that led to a very unfortunate event. My cousin was in need, my family was in crisis, and I am their leader. I wanted to fix it because I am a problem solver, but unfortunately, I was not fully aware of just what situation I got myself into when I simply went to pick up my cousin at the wrong place and definitely the wrong time."

"Alessandra, you do understand that a part of being a good leader is to avoid creating more problems to solve just one," Garrison Wyndham said, his face kind but still concerned.

"I agree, Garrison, I do," she said. "And it is a lesson to be learned for sure, but I think we all have to remember everything I have accomplished in the brief time since becoming cochief executive officer and have some foresight into what I can continue to do."

"And your family issues?" Aldrich asked.

"I have already entered her into a long-term rehabilitation facility," Alessandra said. "I do admit that it will take some good PR and spin to get control of it, and I will take on the cost of doing that, personally. Also, I have been advised by my personal attorney, Ngozi Johns, that the charges will be dropped. Listen, I apologize for the misstep and ensure you all that nothing remotely similar will ever happen again."

"I say we vote. A blind vote," Charlie said.

Alessandra's eyes went to Alek again. He remained stoic. "Without me in attendance?" she asked.

Aldrich motioned to the board's secretary and she quictly moved from her spot next to him to hand Alessandra a notepad with the ADG logo and a pen.

"As a board member, you do get a vote, as well," Aldrich said. "And once you cast yours we do ask you to step outside until we're done."

Ever defiant, she pushed the paper and pen aside. "Of course I vote that I retain my position as co-CEO and executive board member of the Ansah Dalmount

Group," she said, before turning to leave the boardroom. She paced the length of the reception area.

"Ms. Kingsley, come in," Aldrich said into the intercom.

Alessandra gave her a soft smile as she rose to come around the desk and enter the boardroom, softly closing the door.

*Still pretending.*

She had nothing to smile about.

*Forgive me, Daddy.*

"Alessandra."

She turned. Ms. Kingsley beckoned her in.

With a heavy breath, Alessandra strode back inside the boardroom. "And the vote is?" she asked.

"Do not let down those who voted for you to remain, Alessandra," Aldrich said, rising to come around the table and offer her his hand.

She shook it with strength as relief flooded her. "Thank you. Thank you all. I will let not let *any* of you down again," she said.

Alek rose from his seat and stared at her. They shared a brief look before he left the room along with the rest of the board of directors.

Alessandra went to the window to look out at the New York cityscape as Ms. Kingsley walked to the door, as well. Alessandra felt like the weight of the world was on her shoulders, but she stiffened her back, straightened her shoulders and took a long, steadying breath.

"He voted for you to stay, Alessandra," Ms. Kingsley said softly from behind her. "His vote broke the tie."

Alessandra turned from the window just as the

other woman left the boardroom and quietly closed the door behind her, leaving her alone in total shock.

*Alek saved me?*

"Huh?" she said into the quiet of the room, her heart racing. She was at a loss for words and clarity. Her world felt topsy-turvy.

In just an instant everything she thought and assumed to be…wasn't.

Gathering herself quickly, she rushed from the boardroom on her high heels to Alek's office only to find it empty. Feeling an urgency to speak to him, she went to his private elevator and rode it down to the underground parking level, anxiously wringing her hands.

Her heels beat against the concrete floor as she looked at his designated parking spot. It was already empty, and if he had his driver pick him up in the front, she would never make it in time to catch him. The breath she released was harsh as she placed a hand on her hip and shook her head. Her adrenaline caused her heart to pound and her pulse to race as she wondered just why Alek gave up his one surefire chance to oust her from the company.

Alek was waiting in his car at the end of Dalmount Lane in Passion Grove when her Jaguar turned the corner. It pulled to a stop beside him and he climbed from warmth and comfort just as the rear door opened, and she did the same.

He felt like a bundle of pure nerves as the frigid wind whipped around them.

Her surprise at seeing him was clear.

He was just as shaken by the sight of her as he was

earlier when she entered the boardroom. So much so that he couldn't stand to look at her and not rush across the room to embrace her. Kiss her. Love on her.

"Why did you vote for me to remain in my position at ADG?" she asked, her eyes on him.

That surprised him.

"I think you're qualified to do the job, Alessandra," he said. "I have come to value your intelligence, your insight and your vision for *our* company. I want you there to have my back the same way I will have yours."

She lightly chewed at her lips and leaned back against the Jag as she looked up the street and then back at him.

"Forgive me for the time I wasted trying to undermine you," he said, pulling the fitted wool cap he wore down over his ears.

Alessandra looked so unsure. "Thank you for the vote, Alek," she said, offering him a soft and hesitant smile. "But was it because of what we once shared?"

"I don't mix business with pleasure, Alessandra," he told her, his eyes locking on hers as he allowed himself to enjoy the sight of her before him. "Together, you and I are going to make ADG more successful."

They eyed each other, surrounded by winter and almost unaffected by the chill because that simmering chemistry they created was still there, pulsing and waiting to be acknowledged.

"In that second right after I found out you voted for me my mind went back to the night of the party," she admitted, digging her hand down deeper into the pockets of her fur. "And in that same second, I wondered if maybe—just maybe—you really did love me, Alek."

Her eyes were filled with her reluctance to believe in him. That pained him.

He stepped closer to her and reached in her pockets to take her cold hands into his own, rubbing them and warming them, just as he hoped he thawed her heart. "I will *always* love you, Alessandra."

He felt hopeful when her hands tightened around his.

The tears that filled her eyes tore at his soul, but he fought off his impulse to draw her into his arms. He understood that this was her choice, her opportunity to forgive. She had to come to him, not because of his ego but instead because of his acknowledgment of his wrongdoing.

"I stayed outside the police station all night in my car because I couldn't stand the thought of enjoying luxury while you sat in a jail cell," he confessed.

"So that was you I saw leaving this morning?" she asked.

Alek nodded. "I couldn't leave until I knew you were free."

"Wow," she said softly, looking down at their feet.

He freed one of her hands to lightly grab her chin and tilt her head up until their eyes locked once again. "That day on the island, I envisioned you there with me with our kids," he said. "I won't lie. I pushed aside that vision that came to me so easily because I thought I wanted something different, but now I know better, Alessandra."

"Oh, Alek."

"For the last month, I have dreamed of nothing more than you having my babies *and* working beside me to grow our business." He stepped back to drop down to his knee, thankful that the snow had been shoveled off the street.

She gasped at the sight of the five-carat engagement ring he held in his hand.

"I purchased this the day after you left for London and today I know I have to try. I have to ask, even if you say no. I have to tell you how much I love you and ask you to be my forever."

Alessandra came to him and pulled him up to his feet to kiss him softly. "I love you, too, Alek," she whispered in between kisses. "I love you so much."

"Yes, but will you marry me?" he asked, holding up the ring.

"I want it all and I deserve to have it all," she said, holding up her own hand and wiggling her ring finger. "Yes, I will be your forever."

He slid the ring on her finger.

"So the war is over?" she asked, leaning back in his embrace.

"Damn right. From now on it's nothing but love," he answered before he kissed her deeply with a moan of satisfaction.

Alessandra pulled the collar of his coat into her fists as she closed her eyes and kissed him back.

It felt good to be reconnected.

"Congratulations," Roje called out.

Alessandra and Alek broke their kiss to look on as he waved and drove toward the estate away from them.

"Let's go get heated," he said, moving around the car to open the passenger door for Alessandra to climb in.

He hurried to the driver's seat, driving with one hand to hold Alessandra's with the other.

"This is good," she said, smiling at him.

"This is damn good," he agreed.

Soon they were beyond the security gates.

"I live in the main house now," she said.

Alek shook his head. "Not tonight. No way. We have some catching up to do."

"Whatever you say, my love."

He pulled the Bugatti to a stop before the guesthouse. When he left the car, he looked up and spotted her aunt Leonora on her balcony in the distance. She raised her glass of wine to him in tribute before disappearing inside her room and pulling the curtains on the patio doors closed.

Alek helped Alessandra out her car and picked her up to carry inside the cottage to make love to her.

# *Epilogue*

*Eight months later*

Alessandra climbed the steps of the wrought iron staircase to reach the second level of their Georgian manor on the newly named Hope Island. The construction of the estate was complete and now their entire family and some close friends were there with them to celebrate the housewarming and their announcement of a new arrival to the Ansah-Dalmount clan. They were able to have up to thirty family members and friends there at one time.

Everything they envisioned that day as they explored the island had come to fruition.

She pressed a hand against her rounded stomach as she walked out onto the spacious balcony and took in the beautiful view of colorful gardens and extensive lawns.

At the sound of laughter, she looked down at their family enjoying the August weather on the hundred-foot terrace.

Nothing about love and life was perfection, but they were in a good place and happy.

*Thank God.*

Her plan to recover from the scandal of her arrest was effective, and eventually the news coverage of it died down and they were back to normal ADG business again. Plus, the announcement of their engagement had taken prominence anyway.

*No one on the board saw that coming.*

She smiled as her aunt Leonora and aunt Brunela both leaned against the whitewashed railings of the veranda, looking out as Marisa went running off the end of the deck to cannonball into the water with a huge splash. Her cousin had completed her rehabilitation program just a little under a month ago and so far, everyone could see the difference in her. The calm and reliability. She was different. But only time could truly tell. *I'm rooting for her.*

*And so is Naim*, she thought, noticing how his eyes kept going back to Marisa in her swim shirt and boy-cut bottoms, both accentuating her curvy, well-toned figure. After all the turmoil she and Alek put each other through, Alessandra didn't know if she could take another Dalmount-Ansah love match. Especially with Marisa finally in the right headspace to find her true self. *A relationship could be the wrong distraction.*

Samira sat on the middle of one of the thirty lounge chairs on the spacious terrace enjoying the sun beaming down on her bare shoulders in the strapless one-piece she wore, but still tapping away on her computer.

In the seven months since she began working at ADG, the young woman had been on a mission to prove herself. *She reminds me of myself.*

Victor went flying past on one of the Jet Skis.

Alessandra rolled her eyes. After one late night/early morning stroll to the maid's quarters, his wife Elisabetta caught him with his pants down, literally, and reminded him they married without a prenuptial agreement. Once Alessandra made it clear she would not increase his allowance to cover the cost of alimony and child support, Victor curbed his doggish ways. *It seems the only thing Victor loves more than himself is his money.*

"You think they'll notice we sneaked off?" Alek asked as he walked into their massive master suite, already unbuttoning the white linen shirt he wore.

"Who cares?" Alessandra said, turning to lean back against the railing as she awaited her husband.

As the sun set, casting shadows in subtle shades of blues, Alek eased down the straps of her sundress and pressed kisses to her shoulder, clavicles and neck as he exposed her body for his eyes alone. She sighed in pleasure and pressed her hand to the back of his head as he knelt to press kisses to her belly.

"I love you," he said, looking up at her.

"More than I love you?" she asked, stroking his beard.

"Yes."

"Impossible."

* * * * *

# COMING NEXT MONTH
## Available April 17, 2018

### #569 IT MUST BE LOVE
***The Chandler Legacy* • by Nicki Night**

Jewel Chandler's list of boyfriend requirements is extensive—and Sterling Bishop doesn't meet any of them. Sure, the wealthy businessman is gorgeous, but he also has an ex-wife and a young daughter. When steamy days melt into desire-fueled nights, Jewel wonders if he's truly the one for her.

### #570 A SAN DIEGO ROMANCE
***Millionaire Moguls* • by Kianna Alexander**

Christopher Marland, president of Millionaire Moguls of San Diego, is too busy for a personal life. When Eliza Ellicott arrives back in town, he knows no woman has ever compared. A broken heart gave Eliza the drive to succeed, and she's opened a new boutique. Can she trust him again?

### #571 RETURN TO ME
***The DuGrandpres of Charleston* • by Jacquelin Thomas**

Austin DuGrandpre never had a relationship with his father. Determined that his son—put up for adoption without his knowledge—won't suffer the same fate, he tracks him to the home of Bree Collins. The all-consuming attraction is unexpected, but when Bree learns Austin's true motives she faces potential heartbreak.

### #572 WINNING HER HEART
***Bay Point Confessions* • by Harmony Evans**

Celebrity chef Micah Langston's ambition keeps him successful and single. He plans to open a restaurant in his hometown—and that means checking out the competition. Jasmine Kennedy is falling for Micah until she discovers his new venture will ruin her grandmother's business. Has betrayal spoiled her appetite for love?

KPCNM0418

# Get 2 Free Books, Plus 2 Free Gifts— just for trying the *Reader Service!*

**YES!** Please send me 2 FREE Harlequin® Kimani™ Romance novels and my 2 FREE gifts (gifts are worth about $10 retail). After receiving them, if I don't wish to receive any more books, I can return the shipping statement marked "cancel." If I don't cancel, I will receive 4 brand-new novels every month and be billed just $5.69 per book in the U.S. or $6.24 per book in Canada. That's a savings of at least 12% off the cover price. It's quite a bargain! Shipping and handling is just 50¢ per book in the U.S. and 75¢ per book in Canada*. I understand that accepting the 2 free books and gifts places me under no obligation to buy anything. I can always return a shipment and cancel at any time. The free books and gifts are mine to keep no matter what I decide.

168/368 XDN GMWW

Name (PLEASE PRINT)

Address Apt. #

City State/Prov. Zip/Postal Code

Signature (if under 18, a parent or guardian must sign)

Mail to the **Reader Service:**
**IN U.S.A.:** P.O. Box 1341, Buffalo, NY 14240-8531
**IN CANADA:** P.O. Box 603, Fort Erie, Ontario L2A 5X3

**Want to try two free books from another line?**
**Call 1-800-873-8635 or visit www.ReaderService.com.**

*Terms and prices subject to change without notice. Prices do not include applicable taxes. Sales tax applicable in NY. Canadian residents will be charged applicable taxes. Offer not valid in Quebec. This offer is limited to one order per household. Books received may not be as shown. Not valid for current subscribers to Harlequin® Kimani™ Romance books. All orders subject to approval. Credit or debit balances in a customer's account(s) may be offset by any other outstanding balance owed by or to the customer. Please allow 4 to 6 weeks for delivery. Offer available while quantities last.

**Your Privacy**—The Reader Service is committed to protecting your privacy. Our Privacy Policy is available online at www.ReaderService.com or upon request from the Reader Service.

We make a portion of our mailing list available to reputable third parties that offer products we believe may interest you. If you prefer that we not exchange your name with third parties, or if you wish to clarify or modify your communication preferences, please visit us at www.ReaderService.com/consumerschoice or write to us at Reader Service Preference Service, P.O. Box 9062, Buffalo, NY 14240-9062. Include your complete name and address.

KROM17R3

SPECIAL EXCERPT FROM

*Jewel Chandler's list of boyfriend requirements is extensive—and Sterling Bishop doesn't meet any of them. Sure, the wealthy businessman is gorgeous, but he also has an ex-wife and a young daughter. When steamy days melt into desire-fueled nights, Jewel wonders if he's truly the one for her.*

*Read on for a sneak peek of*
***IT MUST BE LOVE,***
*the next exciting installment in*
***THE CHANDLER LEGACY** series by Nicki Night!*

A tap on her shoulder startled Jewel. She turned around and was swallowed up by Sterling's piercing hazel eyes.

"Can I join you?"

Jewel's pulse quickened. She wanted to say no. She couldn't control the effect he had on her. Despite that, she said yes. Sterling eased his fingers between hers and they swayed to the music together. Jewel felt as if she were back in school. Sterling had never been the object of her affection then, but she felt something brewing now.

Jewel physically shook her head to shake off whatever that feeling was. She stepped back, adding space between Sterling and her, then moved in time with the lively beat. Sterling matched her step for step and before long they were engrossed in a playful battle, stirring up memories of old popular dances. Next, a song came on from their senior year. A certain dance was known to accompany the rhythm. Jewel and Sterling joined the rest of those on the floor, moving along with the crowd in unison. They danced, laughed and danced more. Other songs began and ended and the two were still dancing some time later. Dominique and Harper had found partners, too, and were no longer beside Jewel and Sterling.

KPEXP0418

Sweat was beginning to trickle down the center of Jewel's back. Her body had warmed from all the movement.

"Whew! I need a break." Jewel panted, threw her head back and laughed. She hadn't danced that hard in years. She felt free. "That was fun."

"Let's get a drink." Taking her by the hand, Sterling led her off the dance floor and headed to the bar. He asked for two waters and handed one to Jewel. "Want to get some air?"

"Sure." Jewel took the ice-cold water Sterling had just handed to her. She moaned after a long sip. "I needed this."

Sterling took her hand again and led them to the terrace. Jewel was hyperaware of his touch as they snaked through the crowd, but didn't pull away. She liked the way his strong masculine hand felt wrapped around hers.

Once they hit the terrace, the cool air against her warm sweat-moistened skin caused a slight shiver. They maneuvered past people gathered in groups of two or three until they reached the far end of the terrace, which was lit mostly by the silver light of the moon. Jewel placed her hand on the marble parapet and slowly swept her gaze over the sprawling greenery of the country club and what she could see of the rolling hills on the golf course. Closing her eyes, she breathed in the fresh air, exhaling as slowly as she inhaled.

Sterling stood beside her. "Perfect night, huh?"

"Yes. It's beautiful. If my mother were here she would scrutinize every crevice of this place." Jewel turned to face Sterling and chuckled. "She's so competitive."

"So you've gotten it honestly."

"What?" Her brows creased. "Me? No."

Sterling wagged his finger. "I remember you on the girls' lacrosse team. Unbeatable. Let's not forget the swim team," Sterling added. "Didn't you make all-county, and weren't you named the scholar-athlete of the year?"

Jewel blushed. She'd forgotten all of that. "Well. Yes, there's that."

The two laughed and then eased into a sultry silence. Jewel and Sterling studied each other for a moment. The moonlight sparkled in his eyes. Jewel looked away first, turning her attention back to the lush gardens.

*Don't miss IT MUST BE LOVE by Nicki Night, available May 2018 wherever Harlequin® Kimani Romance™ books and ebooks are sold.*

Copyright © 2018 Renee Daniel Flagler

KPEXP0418

Want to give in to temptation with
steamy tales of irresistible desire?

Check out **Harlequin® Presents®**,
**Harlequin® Desire** and
**Harlequin® Kimani™ Romance** books!

**New books available every month!**

---

**CONNECT WITH US AT:**

Harlequin.com/Community

 Facebook.com/HarlequinBooks

 Twitter.com/HarlequinBooks

 Instagram.com/HarlequinBooks

 Pinterest.com/HarlequinBooks

ReaderService.com

**ROMANCE WHEN
YOU NEED IT**

PGENRE2017

Need an adrenaline rush from nail-biting tales (and irresistible males)?

Check out **Harlequin® Intrigue®** and **Harlequin® Romantic Suspense** books!

**New books available every month!**

---

**CONNECT WITH US AT:**

Harlequin.com/Community

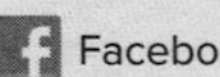
Facebook.com/HarlequinBooks

Twitter.com/HarlequinBooks

Instagram.com/HarlequinBooks

Pinterest.com/HarlequinBooks

ReaderService.com

**ROMANCE WHEN YOU NEED IT**

SGENRE2017

Looking for more satisfying love stories with community and family at their core?

Check out **Harlequin® Special Edition** and **Harlequin® Western Romance** books!

**New books available every month!**

---

**CONNECT WITH US AT:**

Harlequin.com/Community

 Facebook.com/HarlequinBooks

 Twitter.com/HarlequinBooks

 Instagram.com/HarlequinBooks

 Pinterest.com/HarlequinBooks

ReaderService.com

**ROMANCE WHEN YOU NEED IT**

HFGENRE2017R

# lover in you!

Earn points from all your Harlequin book purchases from wherever you shop.

Turn your points into ***FREE BOOKS*** of your choice

OR

***EXCLUSIVE GIFTS*** from your favorite authors or series.

Join for FREE today at
**www.HarlequinMyRewards.com.**

Harlequin My Rewards is a free program (no fees) without any commitments or obligations.

MYR17